THE LUST TO KILL
BURNED IN HIS EYES...

Trotter, the big foreman of the Box L Ranch, hurled himself at Raiford like a charging elephant. Raiford was dazed. Trotter turned and made another rush, but this time Raiford was ready for him. He sidestepped neatly and then came back with a powerful right to Trotter's massive jaw. He worked on Trotter's midsection, his hard fists sinking into the fat body. Trotter fell backwards.

Raiford laughed defiantly and turned to the others. "Any of you scum care to take up where he left off?"

MONTANA MAN

Paul Evan Lehman

LEISURE BOOKS • NEW YORK CITY

A LEISURE BOOK

Published by

Nordon Publications, Inc.
Two Park Avenue
New York, N.Y. 10016

1

Montana Joe Raiford stretched luxuriously beside the twinkling campfire and sighed contentedly. It was nice, he thought, not to have to drag one's blankets into the chill of the chaparral and sleep like a cat lest one be potted like a sitting rabbit. It was comforting to know that here one could get a solid eight hours' shut-eye without being dragged from bed to start on the trail of a killer. All that was over, thank heaven! Here, a couple of thousand miles from the state which had given his nickname, he was no longer the tough, gun-slinging marshal of a hell-roarin' mining camp, but just plain Joe Raiford, a roving cowpoke with enough *dinero* in his belt to buy a little cow spread where he could settle down to a normal humdrum existence.

The fire crackled merrily at him, and he shifted his position slightly and almost purred his enjoyment of its warmth. He had been wise, he told himself, to have quit the game while he was young. It was the ambition to make a stake quickly that had landed him a lawman's job at the age of twenty-three. An ability to handle a .44 Colt swiftly and accurately, plus the nerve to run a bluff when it was necessary, had been all the qualifications he had needed. Miners paid well to have their gold protected and he had saved every cent that it was possible to save. A judicious investment in a tent restaurant had done the rest. At the end of two years he had a strong hunch that he had stretched his luck to the breaking point. Montana Joe believed in hunches. He quit.

Now here he was, stretched beside his campfire, with not a worry in the world and with his whole future before him. He closed his eyes and conjured up a picture of that future. There would be a little ranch in a sunny valley, a staunch cabin, half a dozen good horses, a herd of curly-haired Herefords, a wife —Wife! What in hell did he want with a wife? A dog, maybe, but not a wife. Oh, later on, perhaps; when he got older and a bit tired and lonely—His eyes had popped open at the thought, and now he closed them again.

And then, loud in the stillness of the night, came the boom of a shot.

Force of habit jerked him to an elbow and sent his fingers to the gun which lay close at hand. There came a second shot, a third.

Joe kicked free of his blankets, then deliberately pulled them over him again. You're not Montana Joe, he told himself sternly; you're plain Joe Raiford and you keep your nose out of other people's business. If they wanted to pop each other off in the middle of the night, that was their affair. He stretched out again and forced his muscles to relax. But he still gripped his six-gun.

The desire to sleep had been dispelled by the shots and Raiford resented it. He lay with his eyes open, his head twisted to peer into the shadows which pressed in on him. He became aware of sounds: the distant rustle of brush, the thud of hoofs, faint voices. It was too much. With an exasperated oath he got out of the blankets, drew on his boots and slapped his broad-brimmed Stetson on his head. Then he rolled a cigarette and sat there smoking it, his gaze trying to pierce the darkness in the direction from whence the sounds had come.

The crackle of brush became louder and more definite; somebody was stumbling and crashing through it blindly, desperately. A shadow a bit lighter than its surroundings came into view and resolved itself into the indistinct figure of a man. He approached in weaving lunges to halt swaying with his hand on the trunk of the tree to which Raiford had tied his horse. The thought that the man was seeking a faster means of escape brought Raiford to his feet.

He saw at once that the man had no designs either on the horse or the rope by which it was picketed; he was merely using the trunk for support, and as Joe got to his feet the man staggered towards him, his hands extended beseechingly. When he lurched into the circle of firelight, Joe saw that his face was dead white and drawn and that his eyes held a desperate, hunted look.

"They're tryin'—kill me!" he gasped. "For God's sake hide—!"

He fell flat on his face and lay still.

Raiford crossed to him and rolled him over. His coat fell away and Joe saw blood on his shirt. He felt the man's pulse. Weak; very weak, and rapid. He was a young man with dark hair and not unhandsome features, and in height and build closely resembled Raiford.

Joe got up and turned towards the fire to get his canteen, then halted and turned once more at the sound of breaking brush and the thud of hoofs. He heard a gruff voice say, "There's a fire; reckon he headed for it."

Joe stiffened. There was something familiar in the ring of that voice. It sounded like that of Squat Armstrong. But it couldn't be; not here a full two thousand miles from Squat's habitat. He relaxed, but continued to stand with his back to the fire, the gun in his hand pointed at the earth.

He thought, "If I were still Marshal Montana Joe, this would

6

be my cue to slip back into the brush and get the drop on these hombres when they ride into the light. But I'm not; I'm just Joe Raiford, prospective rancher and man of peace. I stay right here where I am."

The forms of two horsemen materialized out of the gloom and he caught the glint of six-guns as they were jerked up to cover him. The two rode into the clearing and Raiford experienced a tingling of the spine and a freezing of the blood in his veins.

The one was a stranger, a Mexican; but the other Joe knew only too well. The short, powerful torso, the bullet head set upon it without benefit of neck, the mean little eyes and cruel lips, all belonged to the man who had sworn to get him if he had to come back from hell to do it.

The second rider was Squat Armstrong.

Squat was a killer whom Montana Joe had tracked down and had convicted. He had outfoxed and outfought the killer and had earned Squat's undying hatred. It was after the judge had pronounced sentence that Squat had sworn his oath. On his way from the courtroom, manacled to two deputies, he had halted near Joe and had said in his grating voice, "I'll get you for this, Montana Joe; get you if I have to come back from hell to do it!"

Since he was sentenced to hang, it appeared at the moment as though he might have to do just that; but a guard's carelessness had permitted him to escape, the guard paying for his slackness with his life, which Squat's large, gorilla-like hands had squeezed from his body.

Now here he was. Two thousand miles from the scene of his conviction, yet here he was, and for a moment Raiford was overwhelmed by a feeling that was close to panic. Squat's gun pointed squarely at him; his own weapon was directed towards the ground and the slightest attempt to raise it would bring death.

Reason returned swiftly. Joe was standing with his back to the fire and his face was in the shadows. It was evident that Squat had not recognized him or even now the Colt would be spitting fire and lead. He must not be given an opportunity for recognition.

Raiford spoke, pitching his voice a tone lower than normal. "What's the trouble, boys? Who's this fellow?"

The two relaxed slightly, although Squat kept his gun pointed at Joe.

He answered briefly. "Hoss thief. Caught him in the act. Aimed to hang the lousy son, but he broke away and I hadda pot him."

"Well," said Raiford in the same unnatural voice, "he sure

ain't worth hanging now. I just had a look at him. You got him plumb through the chest."

The Mexican kneed his horse over to the still figure and leaned from his saddle to look. The light was dim and Joe's figure cast its shadow across the wounded man, but the splotch of blood on the white shirt was discernible.

"The *señor* ees right," he told his companion. "Thees man ees die okay."

Squat grunted. "Put yore rope on him and drag him off into the woods."

"I don't want him spoiling around my camp," said Raiford. "I know right where to plant him. Little gully I came across when I was looking for water. I'll put him in it and pile some rocks on him." He had to get away from the fire and this was his chance.

He thrust his gun between waistband and body and bent over the wounded man. Keeping his back to the fire, he raised the limp form and swung it over a shoulder and started off into the gloom. He heard them turn their horses and follow him.

He had seen a gully while searching for water, and now he was thankful that its bottom was obscured from the starlight. He made a pretense of roughness, but in reality was very careful as he lowered the unconscious man into the shallow trough. If only the fellow didn't regain consciousness and cry out, he might get away with it.

They sat on their horses watching as he kicked some dirt over the man's legs, then began carrying stones. The heavier ones he piled on the lower extremities, the lighter ones on the chest and arms. Thanks to the darkness he was able to avoid putting any but the lightest on the face, and he was careful to leave space for the man to breathe.

Squat finally said, "That's enough, pilgrim. Whatta you care if the coyotes dig up a lousy hoss thief. Let's get goin', Miguel." He turned his horse and started off at a walk.

The Mexican said, "Much oblige, *señor*, for the 'elp. She's bad *hombre*, thees 'orse t'ief. *Buenas noches*." He raised his sombrero in an elaborate salute and gracefully wheeled to follow Squat.

It was at this point that Raiford was tempted to get the drop on the two and take Squat Armstrong into custody. He conquered the temptation immediately. He would have two prisoners on his hands, one of them a convicted killer who had sworn vengeance against him, and he would have to guard them day and night. He didn't know where the nearest town was located and he might be days on the trail before he could turn them over to the authorities. Even then the chances were that the local law would not be very interested in a man wanted two thousand miles away, or that the Montana authorities would be willing to send that far for Squat. And if he arrested them, Squat would be aware of his presence in this part of the country after he had tried so hard to get away from everything associated with his lawman's past. Better to let the man go. If later they met, Raiford would welcome the shoot-out which would inevitably result. The only difference that would make in Squat's future was that he would die by shooting rather than by hanging.

Raiford walked back to the campfire, listening the while to the diminishing sound of hoofs. He found that he was perspiring and knew that the sweat was not due entirely to exertion. Had Squat caught a glimpse of his face, a familiar note in his voice, he would have been shot down in his tracks then and there. He had no doubt of it.

He sat down with his back to the embers and rolled a cigarette and smoked it. Who was the wounded man? Certainly no horse thief. The very fact that he had been opposed to Squat Armstrong argued in his behalf. Squat had cooked up the story on the spur of the moment to cover the shooting. One thing was imperative: the young man must be gotten to some place where his wound could be cared for, and that as soon as possible.

When Raiford had finished his cigarette the beat of hoofs had been swallowed by distance. He rolled his blankets, got his horse and saddled him, then covered the dying embers with dirt and picked his way through the brush with the horse in tow until he reached a place where he could look out over the silvery rangeland. He could see nothing that resembled man or beast. Squat and the Mexican had most certainly gone their way.

He led his horse to the gully where he had buried the wounded man, and, removing the stones, lifted the fellow from the shallow grave and stretched him out on the ground. With only the light of the stars to aid him, he cut away the shirt and examined the wound as best he could. The bullet had not gone through the chest; it had smashed a rib or two and gouged out a large chunk of flesh. Shock, combined with loss of blood and the exertion, had caused the man to faint.

Joe got his canteen and soaked a compress he made from part of the fellow's shirt with water and bound it in place. As he finished the rough task he caught the glint of opened eyes.

"Take it easy," he said quietly. "You're safe."

"Where are—they?"

"Gone. They think they killed you." He explained what had happened. "Why were they after you?"

"I don't know. Met them in Benson." The young man spoke slowly and with difficulty. "Started for Calixto—with them. Man

9

called Squat picked a fight. When he—yanked his gun, I cut for it. They shot my horse. I landed on my feet and—kept goin'. It was dark, but when I turned to shoot—one of their bullets—got me. I crawled—into bushes—and kept goin'. Saw your fire—and that's all."

"What did you and Squat fight about?"

The young man made a gesture, then whimpered at the pain which followed.

"Nothin' much. Little things. Kept pickin' on me."

"Who are you? Where are you from?"

"Name's Lanier. James Lanier. Father owns ranch in Calixto."

"And you don't know why they tried to kill you?"

"No." The eyes closed again.

Raiford squatted on his heels in the darkness, thinking. Here was a mystery, and his lawman's mind was intrigued. Not even Squat Armstrong would shoot a man without some reason, real or fancied. Evidently Lanier hadn't told everything. Well, it didn't matter. The mystery must remain unsolved. The main thing was to get this young man to some place where he could be properly cared for. With plenty of rest and good food, he'd soon be as good as new.

Raiford said, "I spotted some buildings on the other side of the valley. Probably a little ranch. You'll have to lay up for repairs. If you think you can hang on, I'll put you in the saddle and take you there."

Lanier nodded weakly, and Raiford managed to get him on the horse. He set out across the valley, leading the animal. Every mile or so he was forced to halt for the wounded man to rest, and it was dawn when they finally reached the place. A man was in the yard chopping wood; at sight of them he dropped his ax and came to meet them.

Raiford explained briefly how the young man had been injured. "He says his name's James Lanier and that his father owns a ranch at Calixto. If you can take care of him until he's well enough to travel, I reckon his father'll make it right with you."

The man nodded. "His father'd be Pop Lanier. Owns the Box L. I've heard of him. We'll get the boy inside and to bed; he looks all in. My wife'll take care of him all right."

They helped young Lanier into the house, where an apple-cheeked woman led them to a spare bedroom. They undressed Lanier and put him to bed.

The rancher said, "You'd better stay and have breakfast with us."

"No, thanks; I'll be moving along. How far is it to Calixto?"

"Sixty, seventy miles straight south."

Raiford bade him good-bye and set off at once. He wanted no part of this mystery. The quicker he washed his hands of this, the better. But there was one thing common decency demanded of him; he must stop over at Calixto long enough to report to the boy's father the whereabouts of his son. It was annoying, but it had to be done. Then for the peace and quiet that he craved.

He had yet to learn that the man who'd said there's no rest for the weary had, indeed, spoken quite a mouthful.

2

RAIFORD traveled fast, spending but one night on the trail and arriving at Calixto around midmorning of the second day. Calixto was a typical small cow-town, with the usual single crooked street lined with sunblasted one story buildings, but Joe sensed something brewing as soon as he entered it. There was no tangible indication of trouble, but Joe was aware of it as one is aware of an impending thunderstorm.

During the two years he had served as peace officer, Raiford had formed the habit of noticing details; now as he dismounted before the Royal Flush saloon he saw that there were three other horses tied at the rack and that in front of the general store on the other side of the street stood a double buckboard. He was tired and he was hungry and he was thirsty; of the three, the thirst was easiest to cure. He went into the saloon.

Three men, whom he judged to be the owners of the horses, were at the bar. Two were drinking; the third had turned and hooked a heel on the bar rail and was shaping a cigarette. Raiford automatically took stock of them, thereby continuing another habit of the lawman. The one with his back to the bar was short and stocky and redheaded, with a freckled face and gray eyes. Raiford judged him to be a scrapper, short of temper and aggressive. He saw the reflections of the other two in the backbar mirror as he waited for his glass of beer. They were both lean and rangy, cowhands of the common run. He downed his beer and ordered another. When the bartender fetched it, he asked a question.

"Which way to the Lanier ranch?"

It was as though he had asked the way to Hades. The two cowboys swiveled their heads to look at him; the one rolling the cigarette unhooked his heel and slowly turned, his level gaze meeting that of Raiford in the mirror. The bartender flashed the three a quick glance, then said, "Left fork, six or seven miles south of town." He made a swipe at the bar with his towel and moved away.

Raiford drank his second beer slowly, his lawman's mind asking why these men were interested in an inquiry concerning the Lanier ranch. He put the question aside. He'd probably never know because he wasn't going to linger long enough to find out. He finished his drink and wiped his mouth.

The redheaded man said, "Goin' out to the Box L?"

Raiford turned to face him. "If that's the Lanier spread, yes."

"I don't think you'll like Pop Lanier, pilgrim. He's a mean old cuss, hard to get along with. Now the Double A can use another hand. I'm Mel Thorne, foreman for Abe Ardell. How about signin' on with us?"

"Not interested, thanks."

Raiford faced about and moved towards the door. He heard the clump of boots as the three followed him out.

Across the street, the storekeeper had finished stowing supplies in the buckboard and a girl was untying the team. She was young and undeniably pretty; Raiford saw that, even if his attention was on the three men behind him. They were close on his heels when he reached the rack, and Raiford didn't like it. He swung about to face them.

"You fellows riding in my direction?"

"Nope," answered Mel Thorne. "We're ridin' south and you're ridin' north."

"Guess again. I'm riding south to the Box L."

They were on him like an avalanche, but if they had counted on taking him by surprise they were disappointed. Joe Raiford, man of peace, suddenly reverted to Marshal Montana Joe, gold-town lawman. He sidestepped Thorne, nudging him with a stocky shoulder as he passed. Thorne was thrown off balance and was sent reeling. The second man was stopped with an uppercut to the chin which lifted him off his feet and sent him crashing backward. The third met Raiford with the impact of a boxcar and in an instant they were wrestling all over the sidewalk.

Raiford got a foot behind the other and tripped him, going down on top of him; but before he could make use of his advantage Thorne leaped on his back and locked a forearm around his throat. Thorne tore him off the Double A puncher who immediately added his weight to that of the foreman. When the man who had run into Raiford's fist shook off his daze and entered the fray, Montana Joe went down under their combined weight.

Mel! Sandy! What are you doing?"

The cry came in a woman's voice, and Raiford, twisting his head, saw through the tangle of arms and legs the girl of the buckboard running across the street. Her eyes were glinting and she looked angry, and even in anger she was strikingly attractive. So attractive, in fact, that Raiford, who had never paid more than passing attention to women, found his interest centered upon her rather than the heaving bodies above him.

He saw a smoothly tanned oval face, lips of cherry red, tightly closed, dark eyes that smouldered, a cloud of dusky hair beneath a cream Stetson. All these, and with them the quick, lithe grace of a puma.

He had ceased to resist, there being no point in struggling against the three of them, especially since they were not punishing him but seemed content to hold him on the ground.

Mel Thorne said, "Watch him, boys," and got to his feet as the girl ducked under the hitching rail and stepped onto the sidewalk. Mel said to her, "Just tryin' to persuade this pilgrim that he's headin' north instead of south. He's made up his mind to ride to the Box L and we're unmakin' it for him."

"Let him up."

"Now, Alice, he's just another of them roughs that Pop Lanier's been hirin'. There's been five or six of 'em in the last month, and you know what kind of *hombres* they are."

"Let him up. If he's as tough as you think you can't keep him from going to the Box L short of shooting him."

Thorne gave an angry exclamation and made a motion to the other two. Reluctantly they removed their weight, and Raiford got to his feet and started dusting off his clothes. The girl observed him, frowning.

"He does look tough," said the girl judiciously.

Raiford gave her a level look. "That's because I'm mad. You ought to see me in Sunday school."

"That *would* be something to see," she admitted. "Are you hurt?"

"Just my feelings, Miss Alice."

She started at the use of her name, forgetting that Mel had used it in his presence. The anger in her eyes had died; curiosity shone there now, but before she could speak again, Mel Thorne said,

"Like Miss Alice says, if you're bound to go to the Box L there ain't no way short of shootin' you to keep you from doin' it. We haven't reached the shootin' stage yet, but it's my hunch we're goin' to right pronto. If you sign on with Lanier, and it does come to that, I'll make it my business to be on the lookout for you."

"If I aimed to work for Lanier," Raiford told him coldly, "you sure picked the worst way to make me change my mind. And if you ever do come looking for me, brother, you're plumb out of luck."

"What I said stands," blazed the redhead. "You sign on with Lanier and I'll sure keep you in mind when the fightin' starts."

"Take it easy, Mel," said the girl quietly. "You boys mount up; I'll be ready to pull out directly."

They stamped away to the hitching rail and got on their

horses, leaving Raiford and Alice Ardell facing each other. She was studying him intently.

"Has Lanier hired you to work for him?" she asked.

"Nobody's hired me. I'm my own man and expect to remain that way."

"But Mel said you were going to—" She broke off abruptly and an almost startling change crossed her face. Her eyes widened and brightened, the set lines of her face relaxed, her lips parted in a smile. She spoke swiftly, eagerly. "Then you must be—! But of course you are! I didn't recognize you; but then, why should I? Twelve years is a long time and we were just kids."

Now what, thought Joe Raiford. He'd never seen this girl before; not even in twelve years would he have forgotten her. Before he could put a question there came an interruption. From the far end of the street came a clatter of hoofs, and over Alice Ardell's shoulder Raiford saw her three cowboys freeze in their saddles, their faces turned toward the sound. Thorne said, "Easy!" in a low, hard voice. "Let them start it."

The attention of the girl was distracted also; she turned her head quickly and once more her face tightened. Joe took a look also.

Six horsemen were sweeping along the street in a line which extended from walk to walk. They wore the garb of cowmen and the bold expression of fighting men. Among them one stood out. He was several inches taller than any of his companions and broad in proportion; his big face might have been hewn out of solid walnut, and he had the coarse black hair and keen eyes of an Indian.

The horsemen drew down to a walk and finally halted some twenty feet from the Double A cowboys. All but one of them, that is. At a nod from the big man, a rider on the far side of the street continued to the hitching rack outside the store and dropped from his saddle by the girl's team; and as he did so, Raiford saw him slip the Colt six-gun from its holster.

Thorne and his two punchers sat their horses facing the newcomers, silent, their eyes fixed on the big man before them. Alice stood rigid, lips clamped tight, fingers closed into fists at her side. The big man spoke, his voice a deep rumble.

"Hear you been makin' some brags, Thorne. How about it?"

"I don't brag, Trotter! The word's goin' around that we're stealin' Box L stock. I said that if I heard anybody make that statement I'd call him a liar to his face."

"You can start callin' then. It was me that said it, and I'm sayin'—"

"Mel!" cried Alice as the redheaded foreman stiffened. "Mel, don't do it!" In her anxiety she stepped out into the

14

street. "Don't be foolish! They're six to our three and the man behind the horse has a gun in his hand!"

"You keep out of this, Miss Alice," said Thorne, his gaze never leaving the face of Trotter. "I don't care how many of them there are; I'm still—"

"No, Mel! Please! Don't you see it's a trap?" She turned in desperation to Raiford, her eyes appealing. "Jim! Stop them. They're your men; they'll listen to you."

Raiford blinked in surprise. Jim! His men! What was the girl talking about?

Evidently Trotter wondered too. For a moment his gaze left Thorne to rest questioningly on Raiford. "Jim!" he echoed. "What the hell you talkin' about, girl?"

"Jim Lanier—Pop Lanier's son. Your boss. Newton Cragg found him and he's come back." She turned and walked swiftly towards Raiford. "Stop them, Jim. Can't you see it's just an excuse to start a fight? It would be murder, Jim. My boys haven't a chance."

Raiford had it now. She had mistaken him for James Lanier. He remembered the young man he had saved seventy miles to the north; they were very much alike in build, and a twelve years' absence would account for any difference in their appearance. Well, why shouldn't he be James Lanier for the time being? This was an ugly situation, and the resulting shoot-out would be, as Alice Ardell had put it, sheer murder. Also Joe had taken a strong dislike to the big man, Trotter, and the setup he had arranged.

He spoke crisply. "All right, you Box L men. Get off your horses and come into the saloon. I'm buying a drink."

They were all staring at him now, even the hotheaded Mel Thorne. Then the Box L men turned their eyes questioningly on Trotter. It was evident that they were taking their orders from him.

"You heard me!" snapped Raiford, and there was an edge to his voice now. "Break it up. Get off your horses. You over there—put that gun back where it belongs and come out where we can see you."

The man on the far side of the street came sheepishly around his horse, the gun now in its holster. Trotter glared at Raiford.

"This argument's private and personal," he growled. "Even if you are the Old Man's son you got no right to horn in."

"And you," snapped Raiford, "can't go around settling private and personal business on Box L time."

For a short space their hard glances met and fought it out; but it was Trotter who finally gave in. He swore harshly and spat in the street. "If you put it thataway I ain't got a foot to stand on." He fixed his baleful gaze on the tight-lipped

15

Mel Thorne. "As for you, fellow, when we meet—on my own time—we'll finish this thing."

"The hell with that!" blazed Thorne. "We'll finish it now."

But Alice said sharply, "Mel! The same thing goes for the Double A. No personal quarrels on ranch time."

Mel compressed his lips and sat there glaring, and Trotter spoke briefly to his men. "Come on, fellers. The boss's son is *orderin'* us to have a drink with him."

He slid from his saddle and led his horse to the rack, his angry feet stirring the dust. The others followed and tied, then stalked into the saloon. Raiford felt a light touch on his arm and turned to look down into Alice Ardell's upturned face.

"Thanks a lot, Jim. I was sure I could count on you. The whole thing is such a mess. It's wrong, all wrong. Somehow we've got to straighten it out."

He nodded shortly and went into the saloon on the heels of the Box L men. This was not the time to set her right; he must keep up the bluff until he had delivered his message to James Lanier's father. Then he'd get out of Calixto—fast. What the mess to which she referred was, he could only guess. The Box L and Double A were at each other's throats over cattle thefts of some kind. Open warfare was imminent. Well, the hell with it; it was none of his business.

The men lined up before the bar and Raiford said, "Call your shots."

They were served, and five of the men raised their glasses and nodded acknowledgment to Raiford. Trotter deliberately upended his glass and poured its contents into the sawdust at his feet.

"Gimme another," he said, and slapped a quarter on the bar.

Raiford counted out a dollar and a half and put it on the bar. The attendant glanced at it and said, "You owe another two bits, stranger. There were seven drinks in that round."

"I'm paying for six. You'll have to collect from Trotter for the one he used to wet down your sawdust."

Trotter jerked his head around to glare, and anger changed his face from walnut to redwood. The man standing beside Joe laughed shortly, harshly.

"By jacks, that's tellin' him, Jim. Cough up, Trot; you shore asked for it."

Trotter switched his glance from Raiford to the speaker. "You throwin' in with him, Hurd?"

"I'm backin' him on this deal. Anybody that throws good whiskey away oughta be made to pay for it."

"That goes double with fellers that spill over at the mouth too much," growled Trotter. He slapped another quarter on the bar and stamped out.

Raiford glanced at the man named Hurd. He was slightly

smaller than average, but tough as whangleather. He had a face of stone and eyes every bit as sharp as were those of Trotter. A dangerous man to monkey with, Raiford decided, and a good one to have handy in a pinch.

He said, "Let's go," and led the way outside. Girl, buckboard and Double A cowboys were gone.

The men hung back, evidently expecting Raiford to take the lead. He did so without hesitation. Straight south and then the left-hand fork six or seven miles beyond town. He mustn't miss that fork; it would seem strange to these men if he couldn't find the way to his own home, even—he grinned at the thought —if he hadn't been there for twelve years.

He led the way in the direction from whence the riders had entered town and found that the street ran directly into a trail which was well worn and showed the wheel marks of wagons; and presently he saw ahead of him a small cloud of dust which he decided was made by the girl and her cowboys. If the left fork led to the Box L, the right one must lead to the Double A.

The complications which had arisen since his arrival in Calixto both annoyed and intrigued him. He had come merely to fetch word to Pop Lanier that his son was recovering from a wound some seventy miles to the north and had wound up as the old man's son himself. According to Alice Ardell, he had been away for twelve years. That would make him just a boy when he left. Why did he leave? And why was he now returning? Alice would have been, he judged, eight or nine years old at the time; he could understand now why she had mistaken him for James Lanier. He was the right age and about the same build as the man he had buried and then dug up two nights before. And, of course, his voice would have changed from a boy's treble to a man's baritone.

Well, the deception wouldn't last long. The girl might have been fooled, but Pop Lanier wouldn't be, even if he himself felt in the mood to continue the masquerade. He didn't. He wanted to wash his hands of the whole thing and get going again. He'd take the old man aside and explain briefly, then make tracks. Alice and the rest of them could figure things out as best they could.

The fork in the road was easy to find; it angled off towards a group of buildings in the distance that had to be the Box L headquarters. Raiford turned into it unhesitatingly and the men followed. Nice range, and what cattle they came across were in good condition. These were the cattle that the Double A were supposed to be stealing. The thought of the six cutthroats who rode behind him brought a sardonic grin to Raiford's face. That yarn didn't wash with him any more than

17

did Squat Armstrong's declaration that the young man he shot was a horse thief.

They swung into the Box L yard half an hour later. Five of the six men continued to the corral; Trotter followed Raiford to the low gallery which extended the whole width of the house. There were two men on that gallery. One was fifty or more, thin and hard-faced, who sat with his hands on the arms of his chair staring straight ahead. That, Raiford decided, would be Pop Lanier. The other was of that indeterminate age which might be anything from twenty-eight to forty-five. He was carefully dressed in broadcloth riding trousers, silk shirt and scarf, well-brushed boots, black Stetson hat and cutaway coat.

Raiford dismounted leisurely, allowing Trotter to get to the gallery ahead of him. The younger man was regarding Raiford interestedly; the older continued to stare into the distance before him.

Trotter growled, "Newt, here's that Lanier fellow you've been expectin'."

Raiford mounted the gallery steps and the younger man came forward with outstretched hand.

"How are you, Jim? I'm Newton Cragg, your father's attorney. I'm the man who located you, you know." He took Raiford by an arm and led him to where the older man sat, his fingers tightening and then relaxing in a significant pressure. "Pop," he said, "here's Jim."

Raiford noticed that Pop Lanier was looking in their direction, although there was no expression whatever in his eyes.

"So you've come back, huh?" grunted Lanier.

He did not get up or offer his hand, and his father was turned more towards Newton Cragg than his supposed son. And suddenly Raiford knew why there was no expression in the eyes, why they were not directed towards him.

Pop Lanier was blind.

3

TROTTER was scowling at Newt Cragg. "What I want to know," he grated, "is who gives the orders now."

"Jim, I suppose," answered Newt. "How about it, Pop?"

"I'll give the orders," snapped Lanier. "I ain't dead yet."

"Wish I'd known it. I had Mel Thorne backed up against a wall and was waitin' for him to call me a liar when this feller spoiled the deal."

"What did you do that for?" demanded Lanier heatedly of Joe.

Cragg spoke quickly. "Jim probably didn't know that Thorne and his crew have been stealing Box L stuff."

"I don't know it yet," said Raiford. "I horned in because Trotter didn't think six men to three was big enough odds. He had one of his men hidden behind a horse with a gun in his hand ready to pot Thorne when he made his move. It was a little too raw for me to swallow."

Lanier's face was turned towards him, and it was hard with suspicion.

"That you talkin', Jim? What's the matter with yore voice?"

"It's changed, of course," said Newt promptly. "You didn't expect to hear him chirp in soprano, did you?"

The older man relaxed. "That's right. It would change." The subject of their conversation came back to him and his features hardened again. "About yore hornin' in, you hadn't oughta done it. Rustlers ain't entitled to any breaks."

"I want to be sure they're rustlers first."

"You can take my word for it, can't you?"

"How would you know when you can't see?"

"I got men to do my seein' for me. Good men."

"Now, let's not get into any argument," pacified Cragg. He flashed Raiford a warning glance and shook his head slightly. "Jim doesn't know what it's all about. Come along with me, Jim, and put up your horse and I'll do some explaining."

He made a motion with his head and left the gallery, and Raiford, after a moment's hesitation, followed. Trotter was still within earshot; it would not do to tell Lanier the truth now. He went after Cragg, leading his horse, and Trotter tagged along behind him. At the corral, Newt halted and waited for the two to join him. He spoke to Raiford coldly.

"I don't want you starting any arguments with the old man. That's what busted up you two in the beginning. Give him his way. And in the future don't horn into any plays you don't understand."

"I have a weakness," Raiford told him, "for horning into plays that aren't on the square. If Thorne and the two with him are fair samples of the Double A crew, you'll have a hard time convincing me that they're stealing stock from anybody."

"I'm not going to the trouble of trying to convince you," said Cragg in the same cold voice. "Just sit back in your saddle and take it easy; don't try to push on the reins."

"It's the Ardell gal that give him ideas," said Trotter viciously. "She sicked him on us and he tried to get in solid by showin' his authority."

"So-o-o!" Newt gave Raiford a long, hard look, then spoke to Trotter. "Beat it, you; I want a few words with Mr. James Lanier."

19

The foreman turned away obediently and Raiford's eyes narrowed. Who was this lawyer to be giving orders? And why did the truculent Trotter obey him so unhesitatingly? A sudden violent dislike for Newton Cragg seized him.

"Now get this," Cragg was saying. "I haven't time to tell you the whole story now; I expected to see you in town before you came out. Your mother left the old man twelve years ago and took you with her. She died several years later and you've been knocking around ever since. You saw my ad in a stock journal and got in touch with me, and here you are. I don't think Pop's interested enough to ask about your boyhood, but if he does, dodge the issue until you see me. Understand?"

"I'm beginning to."

"Good. And here's one thing we might as well settle at the start. Jim Lanier and Alice Ardell were kids together, but that was twelve years ago. I've got my location notices on that claim and you're going to keep hands off. If Alice tries to renew the old friendship, give her the brush-off. Do it right at the beginning. You were a kid then; you're a grown man now. It makes a difference. You might even have left a wife up north—Now put up your horse and make your peace with the old man. Remember you're no longer a hotheaded boy. Let him give the orders if he wants to; if we don't like them we can change them. And no romantic ideas about Alice Ardell. That's final. You'll find hay in the barn."

Cragg walked to a horse which was tied to a corral rail and started saddling up, and Raiford eyed him while he stripped his own mount. A sudden decision to sit in this crooked game a while longer had seized him. The whole setup smelled of skunk. Although the lawyer had not admitted it in so many words, his actions and manner suggested that he was aware that Raiford was not James Lanier. He had asked no questions and had demanded no credentials; and that was not the way of the lawyers Raiford knew. And it was he who gave orders on the Box L. Pop Lanier had all the earmarks of being the mean old man that Mel Thorne had represented him as being, but the fact remained that he was blind and helpless. If this slick shyster was trying to put anything over on him, Raiford wanted to know about it.

Cragg swung into his saddle. "Come to my office as soon as you get the chance," he said in farewell. "It's right in Calixto and you can't miss it."

He rode off and Raiford put his horse into the corral, fed him and went back to the gallery. He seated himself near Lanier. "This man Cragg; I suppose you leave most of your management to him."

"No more'n I have to. He's my lawyer. I hired him to find

20

you. You might of saved me that if you'd kept in touch with me. He does what I tell him. When I fired the old crew he found another for me."

"You fired the old crew? Why?"

"They were just settin' around lettin' Abe Ardell steal my stock, that's why."

"How do you know it's Ardell?"

"Proof! Some cows got separated from their calves and went around bawlin' their heads off. Trotter and the boys started lookin' for 'em but couldn't find 'em. Next day they seen one of 'em had got her calf back. That calf was wearin' a Double A brand. I tell you, Abe Ardell's been stealin' our calves and slappin' Double A brands on 'em before we could get around to brandin' them."

Such a thing was possible, thought Raiford; then he remembered Alice Ardell and her boys and decided that in this case it wasn't. He wondered how long Pop had been blind, but did not dare ask.

"Now that I'm here, what do you expect me to do?"

"Put an end to this rustlin'. Do it if you have to wipe out the whole Double A. If you ain't got enough gun slingers to do it, I'll hire more."

"But you're going to give orders?"

"Yes."

Raiford peered narrowly at the hard face. No affection there, no trust or confidence. A son had supposedly come home after twelve years only to find the same callous indifference that had probably driven him away.

"It won't work," he said shortly. "If you're going to hold me responsible for the running down of cattle thieves you've got to let me give the orders."

Lanier turned his head and Raiford saw that his cheeks were slightly flushed. "Just like you used to be—you and yore ma. Stubborn and set on havin' yore own way. I shoulda taken it outa both of you right at the start."

"You can cut out that kind of talk right now. You're the stubborn one, and foolish to boot. If you can't see, how'll you know that your orders are being carried out? As far as I'm concerned, if you're to give the orders you can go ahead and get rid of the rustlers yourself. I'll move on and give you plenty of elbow room."

For once Lanier seemed taken aback. He stared with his sightless eyes, his jaw slack. "You'd—leave me again?"

"In a minute. Without any authority I'd have Trotter and the whole crew pushing me around. I don't need you half as much as you need me. I've done right well on my own." He got up. "I'll take my bedroll inside; you can sit here and think it over."

He went into the house, found an empty bedroom and dropped his blankets on the bed. He was just about fed up with Pop Lanier. He crossed to the window in the rear wall and stood looking out, deep in thought. He saw the blacksmith shop, and in front of it, Trotter fitting a shoe to his horse's front hoof. He rather hoped the old man would stick to his guns, thus giving him the chance to pull out as he had threatened to. The hell with Newt Cragg and his schemes; the hell with Squat Armstrong; the hell with it all.

Still he was intrigued, almost against his will. There were questions running through his mind that cried out for answers. Was Newt Cragg really in love with Alice Ardell, or was the Double A ranch the attraction? Did the lawyer really believe him to be the missing son? If Cragg knew him to be an impostor, why hadn't he denounced him? Was the Double A really rustling Box L stuff, or had the calf been planted for the purpose of making trouble between the two outfits? If so, why?

They were pertinent questions and he found he couldn't dispose of them simply by saying the hell with it. If there were no other reason to hold him, was it his duty to carry on for the real James Lanier who had come so close to passing in his chips? Which brought another question: Had Newt Cragg had a hand in his attempted murder?

His train of thought was broken at the sight of a horseman who at that moment rode into the yard. One glance was sufficient; the rider was Squat Armstrong, and instinctively Raiford stepped back from the window. Squat did not glance towards the house, but walked his horse directly to where Trotter was working. Joe moved forward again, pulled the window catch and stealthily raised the sash a few inches, then knelt to one side of the opening, listening. Their voices reached him distinctly.

"Hello, Squat."

"Hello yoreself. That Lanier feller get here yet?"

"Yeah. He's around on the gallery with the old man. Cocky sonofagun. I had Mel Thorne pinned right down at Calixto and he called me off. That Ardell gal told him to."

"She did, huh?" Squat chuckled throatily. "Betcha Newt won't like that a-tall. I got me a hunch this here James Lanier ain't gonna be among us long."

Trotter looked up quickly. "Why not?"

"Newt got no trespassin' signs posted. Everything set for tonight?"

"Yes."

"Wal, that's what I rode around to find out. Been on a trip up north a ways and just got back. Looked for Newt in town but he wasn't there."

"He was out here."

"Wal, I'll be seein' you." Squat turned his horse.

"Wait a minute." Trotter crossed to Armstrong's mount and stood looking intently up at Squat. He lowered his voice, but Raiford could still distinguish the words. "What's goin' on around here? I don't like playin' games I don't know nothin' about. We're supposed to make war on the Double A; well, that's jake with me. But why? And where does this Jim Lanier fit into the picture?"

Squat leered down at him. "He fits, all right; but don't worry yore brains tryin' to figger how. Just go ahead and do your job and mebbe when it's all over you'll be able to dope out what happened. S'long."

He rode off at a lope, and for a few seconds Trotter stared after him; then he shrugged resignedly and went back to his blacksmithing.

The conversation left Raiford wondering quite as much as Trotter, but he had the answer to one of his questions. The feud with the Double A was being provoked by Trotter and the Box L men. That meant that the calf with the Double A brand had been planted. Was Cragg behind the scheme, or Armstrong? Cragg, in all probability; Squat had plenty of brawn but little brain. Squat seemed to be in the lawyer's confidence, for he knew what it was all about and Trotter didn't. And Squat had been looking for Cragg. To report the death of James Lanier? But that didn't make sense; Newt had been expecting the arrival of Pop's son. And something had been planned for tonight.

Raiford shook his head in bewilderment and softly lowered the window sash. When Alice Ardell had mentioned a mess, she certainly hadn't made an overstatement.

It was nearly noon when he returned to the gallery.

"What do we do about eating?" he asked Lanier.

"Cook fetches me grub from the mess shack. You can eat with the men."

"Thanks. I kind of fancy my own brand of cooking."

He went to the mess shack and got what he needed, then started a fire in the kitchen stove and prepared a meal. When the coffee had boiled he went to the gallery and said, "It's ready; want me to steer you to it?"

"I can find it," answered Lanier, and, getting up, extended a hand before him and walked unerringly to the door. Passing into the house he groped his way to the kitchen, found a chair and sat down. He ate hungrily, seeming to relish the food.

"Best grub I've et for months," he said when he'd finished. His mood seemed to have lightened. "I been thinkin', Jim. I'm goin' to need you. You go ahead and give the orders and I'll cancel 'em if I don't like 'em."

Raiford washed up the dishes, tidied the kitchen and went

23

down to the corral for his horse. He was amazed to see Pop Lanier riding out of the yard on a big bay. Raiford turned to the man who had saddled up for Pop. It was the one named Hurd.

"Do you mean to tell me he rides?"

"Sure. One of us catches up his horse and puts the rein into his hand and off he goes. When he comes back we take the horse and head the old feller towards the house. He gets around right well."

"It's a wonder he don't get lost—on the range, I mean."

"Not with that bay. Eatin'est horse you ever seen. When Pop gets tired of ridin' he gives him his head and he makes a beeline for the feed bin."

"Your name's Hurd, isn't it?"

"That's right."

"Trotter didn't seem to like your siding with me. I figure he's a bad one to cross."

Hurd shrugged. "I ain't losin' no sleep worryin' about it. I've bucked tougher ones than him."

Raiford saddled his horse, mounted and headed directly across the range until he struck the road that ran through the middle of the valley. He followed it to a clump of buildings which he knew must belong to the Double A. As he approached the house he saw a man waiting outside, and when he drew nearer he recognized Newt Cragg. Another surprise! Newt was Lanier's lawyer and the Box L was theoretically at war with the Double A, yet here he was.

It was too late to turn back even if Raiford had wanted to. He rode up to the gallery and dismounted. Cragg came to the steps and glared down at him.

"What are you doing here?"

"Paying a call on a neighbor. Any objections?"

"Yes. I told you—"

Raiford looked past him and raised his hat. "Howdy, Miss Alice."

"Why, hello, Jim." She had just come out of the house.

"Dropped around to talk with you about this rustling."

"Of course." She came forward, stopping at the side of Cragg. "You'll excuse us, won't you, Newt?"

He turned his head to regard her. "You promised to ride with me, Alice, and I've rather looked forward to it."

"But we can ride some other time. This is important."

"Lanier could talk it over with your father."

Raiford said, "I reckon Miss Alice has her father's confidence."

"Which is more than you can say of yours!" snapped Cragg; then at the sight of the astonished disapproval in Alice's face, added, "I'm sorry, Alice, but it's true. I heard Pop tell

24

him that he'd continue to give orders for the Box L."

"Your information isn't up to date," Raiford told him pleasantly. "We made different arrangements. From now on I'm giving the orders on the Box L. Miss Alice, I see you're dressed for riding. Maybe I could take Newt's place. We could talk as we ride."

She nodded her agreement. "Newt, you'll just have to excuse me. I'm sorry, but this feud must stop before it goes any further. Come over tomorrow and we'll have that ride. It's a promise."

"All right." Cragg's face was white and he spoke the words between stiff lips. He came down the gallery steps and the glance he gave Raiford in passing was poisonous. By the time he had mounted he had regained his self-control, and the face turned to them was placid.

"Don't forget, Jim, to stop in at the office the first chance you get. Good-bye, Alice." He raised his hat and rode away.

Raiford got Alice's horse and they swung away together, stirrup to stirrup. He let Alice do most of the talking, noticing the places which she pointed out as having associations with his supposed past. She told him what she knew about the trouble between the ranches, and he learned substantially that Pop Lanier, never a friendly man, had become harsher and more surly and suspicious after his accident.

The accident? Why, Pop had been blasting tree stumps in his northwest forty, planning to put in alfalfa. He had lost count of the shots and a delayed explosion had cost him the sight of both eyes. Maybe his stock was being rustled; maybe, his sight gone, he just imagined it.

The calf with the Double A brand had undoubtedly been planted, probably by Trotter and his men, for most of the trouble had developed after the old crew had been fired. Why had they been fired? Because they refused to believe that Abe Ardell was stealing from his neighbor.

"Alice," asked Raiford, "did you ever hear of a man named Squat Armstrong?"

She shook her head. "No."

"Or a Mexican named Miguel?"

"There's a Mexican named Miguel Rosas who owns a little ranch in the north hills. The Circle Cross is his brand. Why?"

"He's a friend of Armstrong's; I might locate Armstrong through him."

It was nearly five o'clock when he left her at the Double A corral.

She said in parting, "I'm glad you came home, Jim; awfully glad. I'm sure that together we can whip this suspicion of Pop's. You must ride over some evening and have a talk with father. He liked you a lot when you were little. Good-bye."

There was a strange warmness within Joe Raiford as he jogged back towards the Box L. Alice Ardell was all wool and a yard wide. He was in this thing to his neck now, and he couldn't back out. He sighed, but it wasn't entirely with regret.

4

RAIFORD rode into Calixto that night and found without difficulty the office whose sign read, NEWTON CRAGG, Attorney at Law.

The interview with the lawyer, he believed, should be informative; some of the questions which he had been asking himself might be answered. At the very least the interview should be interesting, all the more so because he was going into it blind. He must play his cards close to his chest.

Raiford had tentative answers for some of the questions but he was not yet in possession of sufficient facts to determine how logical these answers were. He must make Newt Cragg talk.

There was a light in the office and he entered to find Cragg seated at his desk. Raiford said, "Here I am," and took the chair which the lawyer indicated. Newt swung his swivel chair to face him, lounged back in a comfortable position and threw a leg over its arm.

"Get it off your chest," said Raiford abruptly, beginning his plan to goad Cragg into talking.

"I will, don't worry. First, how much did Jake Rails tell you before he sent you down here?"

Raiford mentally recorded the name, Jake Rails, and found the proper answer. "Nothing. How much was he supposed to tell me?"

"Just that—nothing."

"Then suppose you start telling me."

Cragg answered coldly. "I'll tell you only what you must know, and that at my own convenience."

Joe sighed. "I'm sorry that I hurried to town just to hear that." He deliberately sought a way to make the lawyer angry; even a lawyer will talk when his brain is seething. "I might have enjoyed a longer ride with Miss Ardell. She's a fine young woman and excellent company."

That got under Newt's skin. He jerked erect in his chair, pulling his leg off the arm and bracing himself as though he were about to pounce. His cold eyes went suddenly hot.

"I told you to stay away from her. I meant it. She's mine."

"That's what you think," mocked Raiford; then as Cragg opened his mouth to berate him, he leaned forward and attacked sharply.

"Listen to me, Cragg. I'm no kid and I refuse to be treated like one. How the hell can I play a game if I don't know the rules? You're as bad as Pop Lanier—wanting to give all the orders, pull all the strings. Well, me and him got together and settled that right pronto; now talk up and tell me what I'm supposed to do. If I know the whole setup perhaps I won't be always crossing you."

"Who do you think you are?" demanded Cragg savagely. His face was red and his eyes blazed with anger. "I want you to remember that your job is to take orders from me, whether you understand them or not. You're being paid for doing just that. I wrote Jake to send me a man I could depend on, and he sent you. All Jake knew, and therefore all you could possibly know, is that your name is James Lanier and that your father owns a ranch at Calixto. You were to report to me here at this office, but I can understand how that mix-up between Trotter and Mel Thorne balled things up. It's a good thing I happened to be at the Box L when you arrived."

"Which proves," said Raiford calmly, "that you should have let me in on the ground floor to begin with. If you hadn't been there I might have made a mess of things."

"How was I to let you know?" asked Newt scornfully. "In writing? You must think I'm a fool! If you had come to the office first, as you were supposed to do, I could have prepared you to meet your loving father."

"You weren't at the office; you were at the Box L."

"You should have waited for me. Has Pop asked you any questions?"

"No. He's just about as affectionate as a clam."

"I didn't think he would; all he wanted his son back for was to take care of the ranch. Now I've told you briefly what happened in the past. Pop drove his wife and son away by his cussedness. He was as mean as sin to both of them. The boy was eleven, and that was twelve years ago; which, in case you can't add, makes you twenty-three. He never heard from them again nor did he make any attempt to find them.

"When he lost his sight in an explosion, I started working on him and finally persuaded him to let me make a search. Well, I located young Lanier and learned from him that his mother had died ten years ago. You're James Lanier, even if your voice has changed." There was a sneer on his lips and he seemed to have regained much of his composure.

"I get it now. But suppose the real James Lanier decides to pay a visit to his father?"

Cragg smiled gently. "You needn't worry about that. He won't appear to embarrass you. I just received a report on him. He started for Calixto on a stolen horse. He was overtaken and killed while trying to escape."

Raiford nodded his understanding. "And where do we go from here?"

"We let nature take its course. You carry on as James Lanier until I instruct you differently."

Well, here was the answer to two of the questions. Newt Cragg knew he was not the real James Lanier, and Newt had engineered the ambush of the young man who was on his way to visit his father.

"I'm still working in the dark. I don't like it. How about this supposed rustling of the Box L cattle?"

"There's nothing supposed about it; they're being rustled. But Trotter will take care of that. You can look to him for orders."

"Like hell I can!"

"Then leave him strictly alone. He doesn't need your help. Just remember that when the job is finished you get $500. That job is simply to be James Lanier. Nothing to do but sit on your tail and take things easy. Pretty soft, isn't it?"

"Not if I find myself sitting in a cactus bed."

"No danger of that. You're sitting in a bed of roses—as long as you keep away from Alice Ardell. As for that—well, just consider what would happen to a beautiful friendship if she should find you're an impostor."

There it was in so many words.

"And think what would happen to another friendship if she discovered it was you who'd palmed off that impostor on a blind old man."

Newt laughed shortly. "Don't be silly. Me do a thing like that? My friend, you wrong me. Alice was honestly deceived, and she knew Jim Lanier when he was a boy; why shouldn't I, who had never laid eyes on him, be deceived also? And it will be me, remember, who exposes him. My stock would rise immediately, Mr.—Lanier. Don't you see that?"

Raiford did. This crafty shyster had him right where he wanted him. Or thought he had. But Raiford held the high trump; the real James Lanier was not dead. He was where Raiford could produce him on very short notice when it became necessary to do so.

He got up. "All right; I'm James Lanier, twenty-three years old and just returned to save the old homestead from the ruthless rustlers of the Double A. Some day in the future I get $500. What happens to me after that is in the lap of the gods—and Newt Cragg. Right?"

Newt gave him a wolfish grin. "Right as rain. Glad to see you're going to play ball. I'll get in touch with you if anything develops. Good night—ah—Mr. Lanier."

"*Adios*, Foxy Grandpa," said Raiford, and left the office.

Well, things were beginning to clear up. James Lanier had

been waylaid and left for dead and a man selected by a certain Jake Rails had been sent here to take his place. Newt knew that he, Raiford, was not James Lanier and believed him to be the one Jake had sent.

That man had not yet arrived at Calixto, and it should prove interesting when he did. It was worth sticking around just to see what would happen with two Jim Laniers on the scene, both of them fakes. But why was the presence of a son necessary at all? Raiford thought he had the answer to this one, but time alone would tell whether that answer was the correct one. If his hunch was right, old Pop Lanier was in deadly danger. He'd have to string along with Newt until he was sure.

And he must leave Alice Ardell strictly alone. To this jackal? Not in ten million years. He'd get the goods on this crook and show him up for what he was. Making Newt mad was one way of bringing him out into the open, and Raiford could find no better way of angering the man than by seeing Alice just as often as he could.

It was late when he reached the Box L and Pop Lanier had gone to bed, but the door of the lighted bunkhouse was open and he could see four of the men playing poker. Trotter was one of them. Raiford walked completely around the building on his way to the house, and saw that there was no rear door. If Trotter left the place that night it must be by the front. Joe placed a chair on the gallery where he could see both bunkhouse and corral and waited in the darkness.

After an hour or so the light was extinguished, the door shut, and stillness descended. Midnight came and Trotter had not left the bunkhouse. Another hour and Raiford became uneasy; whatever had been planned for the night should be under way by this time. Quietly he made his way to the crew's quarters.

For a full minute he stood outside the door listening to the chorus of snorts and snores from within. There wasn't a single indication that its occupants intended leaving the place before morning, yet he knew definitely that something had been planned for that night.

Frowning in perplexity, he made his way to the corral and whistled softly. His horse came in answer to the signal and he led him through the gate and saddled up. He didn't know where he was going, but a disquieting feeling that things were happening somewhere on the spread had seized him. On the theory that if cattle were to be rustled it would be at some point remote from the house, he headed south, walking his horse.

He came presently to the fence which separated the Box L from the Double A, turned west and followed it. It was very quiet and the only moving things besides himself and his horse were the occasional cattle which got up and lumbered out of his path. He drew up at last on the bank of the creek which ran through the valley. His horse lowered its head and drank.

On the far side of the creek a ridge paralleled the stream and Raiford's eyes followed its outline half a mile beyond the fence; and suddenly he turned in the saddle and his gaze remained fixed. A horseman had topped that ridge, hung for a moment against the sky, then dipped into the shadows. Close behind him followed a steer, then another, and finally a thin column of them. Joe saw the forms of two more riders, probably flankers, then more animals, and eventually two horsemen who brought up in the drag.

Raiford jerked his horse to the left and sent him scudding to the fence. Dismounting, he snipped the wire with his pliers, led the horse through the gap, then hastily remounted and set out at a soft canter towards the spot where the drive must cross the creek.

To his left another ridge showed itself, shrouding the creek in the deepest gloom. When he heard the sound of splashing water where the animals were being hazed across the stream, he pulled down to a walk. So dark was it that he was almost on the drive before he saw it.

He made out first the shape of a horseman directly before him. The man was facing the other way, hazing the steers onward as they left the water. Presently this rider turned and rode along the flank on the drive without glancing in Raiford's direction, and Joe immediately urged his horse forward until he occupied the position the fellow had just vacated. When he could hear the voices of the two drag riders he swung his mount and fell in beside the column. If he maintained this position there was a chance that the rider ahead would think he had come up from the drag while the two behind would mistake him for a flanker.

He crowded his horse against a steer and, leaning over, ran his hand across the animal's flank. His fingers found the scar of the brand and traced out the shape of a Box L. These were Lanier cattle, all right, and they were on Double A range. But they were not being driven by Box L cowboys.

His horse was climbing steadily, and Raiford saw the head of the column top the ridge, hang there against the sky, then drop over the summit. The darkness was losing its intensity as he climbed nearer the crest, and Joe found himself wondering if the two in the drag would notice that four men preceded them instead of three. One of the flank riders passed safely over, then the second one was outlined against the sky. And then all hell broke loose.

Rifles and six-guns crashed in a scattered, thunderous volley; he heard hoarse yells from somewhere along the creek and the whisper of flying lead was all about him. Raiford saw the man at the top of the ridge jerk in his saddle and heard his cry of pain above the welter of other sounds.

Things were happening so swiftly that the mind could not catalogue them individually. He heard the bawl of cattle and knew the animals were scattering in all directions; the two drag men were cursing and firing into the blackness which hovered over the creek; hoofs pounded and lead whined; he saw figures of mounted men flashing across the ridge at an angle in an attempt to cut off the leaders; he knew more mounted men were charging in from the side.

He brought his horse to a halt, held him there as he pranced nervously. A drag rider nearly collided with him, pulling his horse to its haunches and spinning it on its hind feet to avoid the crash, and for an instant Joe saw a burly body against the sky and knew it for that of Squat Armstrong. Then came a gruff oath and the words, "What in hell you waitin' for? *Look out!*"

A horse came plunging out of the darkness and struck Raiford's mount on the shoulder, sending it reeling. Squat's horse leaped nervously to one side and Raiford's mount went down, throwing him heavily.

"Stand hitched, you!" the one who had crashed into Raiford called, but Squat did not obey. His gun roared from saddle level, and Raiford, lying helplessly on the ground, saw the other slump; then, as his horse shied to one side, slip to the earth. Instantly Squat wheeled his horse and sent it bounding for the crest of the ridge.

Raiford got to his knees, reaching for his gun. It had slipped partly from its holster and he was two seconds getting his fingers about the butt. Those two seconds spelled the difference between life and death for Squat; by the time Raiford had swung the weapon into line, Armstrong was an indistinguishable blur in the gloom.

Noises were all about Raiford—the thunder of stampeded cattle and of horses' hoofs, excited yells, the roar of guns. His horse had scrambled to its feet and Raiford leaped up and caught the rein before it could bolt. He fought it to a standstill, swearing softly and wondering who Squat had shot and whether he still lived. Then he heard hoofs pounding towards him and knew that he must run for it or shoot.

He moved silently away, dragging the nervous horse after him. If he were found here beside a dead Double A man they would hang him out of hand. He angled down the slope towards the point where the fence crossed the creek, and not until he reached the stream did he venture to mount. He glanced back as he swung into the saddle and saw a pin point of flame spring into being and hover over the stricken Double A rider.

The protection of the ridge on his right was lost by the time he reached the fence, and he was passing through the gap he had made when a chorus of yells told him he had been spotted. The roar of guns followed at once, but the light was poor and he was not hit. He didn't linger to fasten the wire behind him, but turned eastward and put spurs to his horse.

His pursuers could not angle to head him off without having to cut the wire, so he had a comfortable lead when they finally rode through the gap and onto the Box L range. Not knowing the lay of the land, he had to ride it blind, and it seemed an eternity before he hit the fringe of timber and found sanctuary among the trees on the east side of the valley. As soon as he was screened from sight, he cut northward, and after a short dash pulled the horse to a walk and finally halted him behind a clump of brush.

He heard the crash as the Double A riders broke into the woody barrier, and caught the sound of their angry voices as they forged ahead into the timber. They would not be deceived long; suspecting the Box L crew as they must, they would move directly for ranch headquarters as soon as they were sure they had lost contact. Raiford spurred his mount to a lope, dodging in and out among the trees, hoping that the sounds he made would be lost to them beneath the noise of their own progress; and at last he edged out onto the open range and, crouching low in his saddle, put the animal to its best pace.

When he came in sight of the house he halted, dismounted and stripped the gear from his wet horse. Smacking the animal on the rump, he sent it off at a trot, then shouldered the gear and trudged swiftly to the gallery. Very quietly he entered, for while Pop Lanier was blind he was not deaf. Carefully lowering his gear to the floor of his bedroom, he stripped off his outer garments and got into bed. He was there less than ten minutes when they arrived.

There was nothing stealthy about their approach; the Double A crew came thundering into the yard and pulled up before the bunkhouse. There followed a bedlam of voices in which he recognized the gruff tones of Trotter and the sharp, angry voice of the redheaded Mel Thorne.

From the other bedroom came Pop Lanier's querulous voice. "Jim! What in time's goin' on out there?"

"I'll go out and see," he called in answer, and got out of bed.

He drew on his boots and trousers and went outside, making all the noise he could. Down at the bunkhouse a light was burning and men were milling about the entrance. As he ap-

32

proached he caught the glint of moonlight on weapons and saw several of the Double A men covering the bunkhouse door. He strode boldly among them and stepped through the doorway.

"What's going on here?" he demanded in his hardest voice.

Trotter stood in the middle of the floor in his underwear, his hair disheveled, the picture of a man suddenly and rudely awakened from deep sleep. Facing him was Mel Thorne and another Double A puncher. Mel's freckled face was as red as his hair and his short form was rigid and menacing. The rest of the Box L men were in their bunks, some sitting up, others leaning on elbows. Their faces reflected anger and mystification.

"We're lookin' for a skunk!" blazed Thorne, his hot gaze still on Trotter.

"Don't talk in riddles, Thorne. What's all this fuss about?"

Thorne wheeled to face him then, and Raiford saw by the light of the hanging lamp that his eyes held anguish as well as anger in them.

"All right, I'll put it in words you can understand. Not more than an hour ago some lousy son shot and killed Abe Ardell. And the polecat that did it is right here on the Box L!"

5

"THAT'S A LIE!"

Trotter blurted out the words, standing there in the open in his underwear and without a weapon. Mel Thorne wheeled, his gun whipping up, but he did not fire. The blazing eyes of the Box L foreman, his anger-reddened face, his very fearlessness bespoke sincerity.

"It's truth! Abe's lyin' out there on the range right now. And he's dead—shot through!"

Trotter made an impatient gesture. "I ain't doubtin' that. But when you say the feller that done it is here in this room, you lie! We were all abed by ten o'clock and not a man has stirred out of his bunk since."

"That's right, Thorne," said the man named Hurd. "A cat couldn't slip out of this bunkhouse without wakenin' me."

"And who are you to alibi them!"

Hurd's eyes hardened, but his voice was quiet. "I ain't no party to murder; you can tie to that."

Thorne studied them each in turn, his red rage turning to uncertainty. Once more he faced Raiford. "If none of them are guilty, that leaves you and the old man. And he's blind."

"Do I look as though I'd been galloping around shooting

people within the past hour? Thorne, you've made a serious accusation; what have you got to back it up?"

Thorne drew a deep breath, obviously holding himself under restraint.

"We've been night ridin' lately in order to try to pin this rustlin' where it belongs. Tonight we spotted a little bunch of cows bein' driven by five men. We jumped them and there was a mix-up. One of them shot Abe, and we chased him over onto the Box L range and lost him. In the meantime one of our boys had roped a critter and found it wearin' a Box L brand. Those cattle were bein' driven on our range to make it look like we rustled them."

"That's just guesswork, Mel. If you lost the fellow you don't know where he came from originally. Maybe he headed for Box L range to mislead you. I'll take an oath that there isn't a man of the Box L crew who hasn't been asleep for hours."

"Would that oath include Jim Lanier?"

"It would," answered Raiford promptly, knowing that James Lanier was at that moment sixty miles away.

A querulous voice spoke from the doorway. "What's all this racket about? Can't a feller get any sleep around here any more?"

Raiford turned to see Pop Lanier standing in the doorway. He wore only trousers and boots and he had one hand on the door frame. The sound of voices must have guided him from the house.

Trotter said, "Mel Thorne comes bustin' in here claimin' that one of us shot Abe Ardell. I told him that's a lie."

" 'Course it's a lie. Maybe I can't see, but there's nothin' wrong with my ears. Not a man has been off this spread to-night."

Thorne gave an exasperated oath. "We're just wastin' time. Boys, take a look at the saddles and the horses in the corral." He brushed past Raiford and Lanier and strode towards the saddle shed. His men followed him.

Trotter growled, "Let the danged fools look. I'm goin' to bed. Jim, put out the light and steer Pop back to the house."

Raiford extinguished the light and took Pop by an arm. "Come on."

Outside the bunkhouse Lanier whispered, "Where's yore hoss?"

"Where do you suppose?"

"You'd be a fool to turn it into the corral."

"They won't find a wet horse of mine in that corral."

"Abe's really dead?"

"Mel Thorne says he is."

34

Lanier chuckled. "Good work, boy!" He patted Raiford on the arm.

Joe was startled. "What's the idea?"

"Now don't get yore brains in an uproar. Like I said, I can't see but my hearin's all right. I lied to Thorne when I said nobody'd been off the spread tonight; but I'm yore father, ain't I?" He cackled again.

Raiford said nothing. Evidently Pop had heard him leave or enter the house despite his efforts to make no sound. Lanier believed that he had shot Abe Ardell, and for the moment he must let him think so. He steered Pop to his bedroom and went into his own. Outside he heard the Double A men moving about in the saddle shed and the corral, but after a while they rode away and silence descended on the Box L.

Raiford did not go to sleep at once, but lay there reviewing the events of the night and trying to foresee those to come. The news that the dead man was Abe Ardell had hit him like a poleax. Ardell, owner of the Double A—father of Alice! And the slightest mistake on his part, the finding of a single little clue by Mel Thorne, would stamp him as Ardell's murderer!

He realized suddenly how deeply he was enmeshed—he, who had determined to keep out of this thing at all costs. Mel Thorne firmly believed that the Box L cattle had been driven by Box L men, regardless of their alibis. Joe knew they hadn't. He even knew who one of the drivers was. But he couldn't divulge the information now. He had fled from the scene, and they had chased him. Nobody knew Squat Armstrong by name or by reputation; an accusation at this late date would be laughed at. They'd hang him higher than Haman and Newt Cragg would be free to pursue whatever iniquitous plan he had cooked up.

Raiford thought a bit further. Alice must believe that her father was killed by somebody on the Box L. He wondered if her mother was living and if she had brothers and sisters. If she was the only child, then she would practically own the Double A. And Newt Cragg wanted to marry her, thereby acquiring the ranch. Squat Armstrong had fired the fatal shot; had it been part of Newt's plan?

He pondered it and finally decided that it hadn't. The whole thing had come about suddenly, a surprise to the rustlers; there was no means of Squat's knowing that the man who had come charging out of the blackness at him was Abe Ardell. He doubted if Squat had even recognized the man he had shot. No; Abe Ardell's shooting had been an accident, but a fortunate one for Cragg.

A deep anger against Squat Armstrong began burning. Squat was a murderer twice over and the man to bring him to account was Montana Joe Raiford. He would set about tracking

35

down the fellow at once. Miguel Rosas knew him, and Miguel owned the Circle Cross in the hills. It must have been Miguel's men who had been driving the cattle. That knowledge suggested several theories, and Joe proceeded to investigate them.

The first and simplest one was that Rosas was working for himself, stocking his ranch from both the Box L and Double A, allowing the two outfits to blame their losses on each other. The second and more logical, because there was a definite connection between Squat and Miguel and Newt Cragg, was that the lawyer had a financial interest in the Circle Cross. The trouble with both theories was that there was no room in the setup for James Lanier. Newt had gone to considerable trouble to locate young Lanier, then have him removed, then plant a substitute on the Box L. No, there was a deeper significance to the thing, and Raiford's original hunch was slowly taking the shape of a third theory, as yet so hazy and bizarre that Raiford refused to consider it until he had gathered in a few more loose ends.

Pop Lanier was quite cheerful at the breakfast table the next morning, and Raiford saw with a feeling of disgust that the old man actually relished the knowledge that Abe Ardell had been killed.

"How'd you do it?" he questioned avidly. "Catch 'em rustlin' some of our cows?"

He had not reached the bunkhouse in time to hear Mel Thorne's story, and Raiford repeated it for his benefit.

"It wasn't Thorne's men who were driving those cows. They wouldn't have jumped their own men. And I didn't shoot Abe Ardell. I was there when it happened and I'd have been blamed if they'd caught me. That's why I checked out so fast."

The old man fastened blank eyes on him and cackled with amusement.

"You're a slick *hombre*, Jim; slick as all get-out. You jest stick to yore story. But you can't fool yore old father. Abe's men was drivin' them cows, all right; but of course Mel couldn't admit that. My guess is that you potted one of them drivers from the brush and it turned out to be Abe. Serve him danged right."

Raiford got up from the table. "Have it your way," he said shortly. "You're all wrong, and it isn't just your eyes that are blind. I'm riding to Calixto."

"What fer?"

"To see if I can scare up some flowers for Abe's funeral."

The old man cackled again. "Nice goin', boy! Gotta be a good neighbor, hey? Kills suspicion."

Raiford went out muttering to himself. The more he saw of this wicked old man the more he was inclined to sympathize with the wife and son who had left him twelve years before.

36

By the time he had saddled up some of his anger and disgust had vanished. Here was a man who could not see, who had to do his thinking in continual darkness; a man who, had he normal vision, would have read in the visages of those who worked for him the kind they really were: hired gunmen, greedy for the high pay they undoubtedly received, disloyal, willing to commit any crime for monetary gain.

He found Calixto seething when he entered it; no longer was there just the hint of coming storm in the electric atmosphere, the lightning had already struck. There were men standing on the corners and in doorways, talking in low voices. Abe Ardell was well known and well liked. Hostile glances followed him as he rode slowly down the street, glancing to right and left for some sign of a flower garden.

Near the end of the street he spotted one, its colors showing in a bright patch behind a cabin. He dismounted and walked around the house. A woman was cutting blooms with a pair of scissors. The one for whom she was cutting them was Newt Cragg. Newt looked at him as he approached.

"You wanted to see me, Jim?"

"No. I'd like to buy some posies if the lady will be kind enough to sell them to me."

Newt frowned. "What for? Under the circumstances, flowers from the Laniers would hardly be appropriate."

"Ardell wasn't shot by anybody from the Box L. You ought to know that."

The woman moved on down the row, selecting her flowers. Newt lowered his voice. "I think I'm going to have trouble with you."

"Try pinning any murders on me, and I'll guarantee you will."

Newt gave him another hard look, which was returned with interest, then wheeled and walked away.

The Double A ranch was a scene of gloom. The big house was silent and brooding; the cowboys moved aimlessly about on various little tasks or sat in somber quiet on the bunkhouse bench. Mel Thorne stood near the corral, hands shoved behind his belt, gazing frowningly into empty distance. He was essentially a man of action, and nothing is so galling to such a one as the knowledge that he is completely tied and unable to move.

The cattle which were found on the Double A range were Box L cattle, and the assumption was that they were driven by Box L men, for one of these had been chased over Box L range and had been lost on the Box L side of the fence. When Mel had led his men into the yard it was with the full assurance that some evidence of their guilt would be easily found. But he hadn't found a thing. The men had every appearance of having been asleep for hours; there were no wet horses in the corral or damp saddles on the rack. To assume that each man had another horse and another rig which he had secreted on his return would be stretching it too far even for the impulsive redhead. He was convinced that the cattle were to have been planted on the Double A range, but he had absolutely no proof. He was certain that Abe Ardell had been shot by somebody from the Box L, but again he had not the slightest bit of proof. So he simmered in his own rage, impotent but willing and anxious to fight at the slightest excuse.

There were visitors at the Double A that afternoon, for Abe Ardell had many friends. Among the visitors was Newt Cragg. He bore a simple floral tribute and his attitude was one of grave and sympathetic solicitude. As he rode slowly from the yard he met Joe Raiford riding in. Neither man spoke to the other, but Newt was scowling as he continued towards town, and his muttered oath reached Raiford's ears and brought a grim smile to Joe's face.

The holster at Raiford's side was empty, although there was a rifle in the boot beneath his leg. Several of the Double A crew glared at him, and Mel Thorne turned away from the corral and came striding purposefully towards him.

Raiford dismounted outside the house, dropped a rein over the hitching rail and waited for Thorne. The Double A foreman spoke heatedly.

"What do you want?"

"I rode over to pay my respects to Miss Alice," Raiford told him quietly. "It's the very least I can do."

"You sure got gall!" Thorne said it bitterly, and his fingers were opening and closing as though itching to snatch at his gun.

"I know how you feel. I also know that nobody from the Box L shot your boss."

"Like hell they didn't! And you pull a long face and come crawlin' over here to cover up for 'em. Well, I reckon I can speak for Miss Alice and her mother and say your sympathy ain't wanted."

A voice came from the doorway. "Who is it, Mel?"

"You got comp'ny. And he's playin' it safe by comin' without his gun."

She came out on the gallery slowly, her gaze on Raiford. "What is it?"

There was no friendliness in the question, neither was there animosity; the words were flat and expressionless.

Raiford took off his hat. "I just had to tell you how sorry I am. I know there's been trouble between the two outfits, and now I guess there'll be more. But just the same I had to come over and tell you."

"Thank you," she said in the same flat voice.

"I—brought a few flowers." He went back to his horse and untied the thong which bound the bouquet to the saddle. He removed the newspaper in which they were wrapped and, returning to the gallery, handed them up to her.

Her gaze faltered before his steady regard. "They're very nice," she whispered.

Thorne spoke harshly. "Now that you've spoke your piece and handed over your flowers and got thanked for your sympathy, get the hell out of here and get out fast."

Raiford continued to look at Alice, his eyes begging for understanding; but she returned his gaze without warmth and finally he turned and took the rein from the rack. Raising himself into the saddle, he looked at her again.

"You won't believe me, I know; but no matter what the Box L might have done in the past, I give you my word that none of us fired the shot that took your father from you. That's God's truth, Miss Alice."

"Yeah, it is!" said Thorne scornfully. "Don't let him soft-soap you, Alice. Go on, Lanier; make tracks."

Raiford touched his hat and turned his horse. Slowly and gravely he rode from the yard. His heart was heavy. She had not said so, but she believed the Box L guilty. Well, why shouldn't she?

There was, he decided, but one thing to do. He must find Squat Armstrong and choke the truth out of him, or pin the slaying on him so irrevocably that he could not squirm out of it.

He reached down and got his gun out of his saddle pocket, tested its action briefly and pushed it into his holster. The rifle he would use for long range work. When he went through the gate in the fence, he turned eastward and followed it as he had followed it the night before; but when he reached the base of the hills he sent his horse straight ahead, climbing steadily.

Somewhere in those hills was Miguel Rosas' Circle Cross ranch, and there, he was convinced, he would find his man.

6

RAIFORD did not know the location of the Circle Cross, but Alice had told him that it was in the north hills. The two ranges which bounded the valley ran roughly north and south, but he headed for the one on the east side since it was in that direction the cattle drive was headed the night before.

He followed approximately the same course he had taken when he was pursued, but when he entered the timber he did not turn northward at once, but continued upward until he found a path leading towards the summit. This he followed, climbing constantly, until the path joined a road which paralleled the crest. Cattle had passed over this trail and Raiford was practically certain that the Circle Cross had been their destination, thus confirming his belief that Miguel Rosas was the one actually responsible for the rustling.

He turned north on this road, advancing with caution. He had every reason to be wary, for somewhere in these hills was the man who had sworn to kill him and who, he knew, would attempt to carry out his purpose on sight. Twice the darkness had saved Raiford from recognition, but it was daylight now. He scanned every rock and gully that might conceal an enemy and made detours to avoid them. He carried his rifle across his knees.

There was no interruption to his progress, but the feeling that he was being watched gradually seized him, and finally his gaze went to a distant peak in time to catch the flash of the sun on the lenses of field glasses. Miguel Rosas quite evidently took precautions to prevent surprise.

It was after noon when he topped a ridge and found himself looking down into a little park where cattle grazed and where the presence of buildings indicated that this must be headquarters for Rosas. Beyond the buildings rose the peak from which he had been watched.

Raiford rode slowly into the basin, his eyes noticing the cattle as he passed. All of them that he saw wore the Circle Cross brand. As he neared the buildings he pushed the rifle into its boot and made sure that his six-gun was loose in its holster. If Squat Armstrong were here the action would be at close quarters, fast and furious.

A single Mexican sat on the ground outside an adobe hut with his back to the wall, his knees hunched up, his sombrero drawn over his eyes. His right arm was in a sling and Raiford wondered if he had been the man riding flank who had been injured the night before.

His probing glance took in every inch of the place—the doors and windows of each building, the spring wagon whose bed might hide an enemy, the haystack, the adobe wall around the well. As he approached, the Mexican raised his head and pushed his sombrero back.

"*Buenos días,*" he greeted sleepily.

Raiford halted his horse, his glance still flitting about the place.

"Where's everybody?"

The Mexican made a gesture which embraced most of the

surrounding land.

"Where's Rosas?"

"*Quién sabe?*"

Raiford leaned forward in the saddle. "Where's Squat Armstrong?" Then, as the Mexican gave him a blank stare, "The big American; the friend of Miguel."

The man shook his head. The *señor* was mistaken; there were no *Americanos* on the Circle Cross. He did not know the man.

"What's the matter with your arm?"

"I'm clean the gon; she go off—*bang*."

Raiford grinned his disbelief and stepped out of the saddle. "I'll take a look around."

The Mexican shrugged indifferently, pulled his hat over his eyes and once more settled back against the wall. He appeared to go to sleep immediately.

Raiford made his search. It was thorough but fruitless; there wasn't a soul on the place but the somnolent Mexican. He finally remounted and set off around the base of the peak, believing that whoever it was who had been watching him had left his post by this time.

When he had described a quarter circle around the base of the peak he came to a gap through which he could see another small park with a log cabin in it. He rode warily into the basin and headed for the shack. Its door stood open, and since there were no windows in the front a shot could reach him from the interior only through the one opening. As he approached it he heard a faint shout and glanced quickly to his right. Through another exit to the park he caught sight of three horsemen driving some cattle.

He rode to the doorway, gun in hand, eyes stabbing about in search of movement. There was none. He dismounted and moved to one side of the door, scanned the interior briefly, then crossed to the other side and looked into the cabin from a different angle. At last he stepped inside, the gun held rigidly at waist level.

The cabin was empty.

There was but the one room, with no possible hiding place except beneath the bunk. He stooped and looked under it. No one there. He went out and mounted his horse and was about to ride away when there came to him distinctly the sound of a heavy thump. It was as though a solid object had fallen to the floor from the height of say a table. He checked his horse and listened. The sound was not repeated.

He circled the cabin at a short distance, then wheeled his horse and raced around it in the opposite direction. No one was playing tag with him. Mystified, he again dismounted and went into the cabin. It was as empty as it had been before.

There was a stool and several boxes, but they were upright; there was a table and on it a bottle with a candle stuck in its mouth, but it stood erect; there was a stove with a teakettle and some skillets, but none had fallen to the floor. There were also dishes on a shelf behind the stove and several heavy coffee cups, and none of these had been disturbed. There was nothing that he could see which could have caused that heavy thump. Yet he had heard it.

Raiford shook his head perplexedly, then went out and got onto his horse. He headed for the other exit, spurring to a lope. Whatever the noise had been it had not been made by Squat Armstrong. Squat would not hide; he'd come out shooting as soon as he recognized Montana Joe.

He raced through the cleft in the basin wall, watching warily for an ambush. He was in rustler territory and his approach had been observed; Squat would not be his only enemy. A spur of hill hid horsemen and cattle from his sight, and he urged his horse to its best pace. After several miles of twisting progress he rounded a bend and come upon them. There was a rider on each flank and a third in the drag. From their costumes he knew them to be Mexicans. He reined in behind the one in the rear. He was undoubtedly the one who had been with Squat the night James Lanier had been shot.

"*Buenas tardes*," said the Mexican. "You are 'urry to go some place, no?"

The man was dark and slender, and his teeth flashed beneath very black, very neat *mustachios*. The eyes were black and probing. A clever rascal.

"Where's Squat?" asked Raiford abruptly.

Miguel had reined his horse about so as to face Raiford. He assumed a puzzled look. "Who you say?"

"You know who I mean. Squat Armstrong. He's a friend of yours."

Miguel shook his head. "The *señor* ees mistake."

"I don't think so. He's a big American with a bullet head and a short neck. Dark and mean-eyed. Strong."

"No such is frien' of Miguel Rosas."

Raiford was silent for a moment. To say, "I'm the one who buried the fellow you and Squat shot," would gain him nothing but, possibly, a bullet in the back. He might get that anyway if the keen eyes of Miguel recognized him.

"I could be mistaken," he finally admitted grudgingly. "I'm anxious to find Squat and a friend of yours told me you'd know where he is."

"W'at frien'?"

Raiford made a stab in the dark. "Newt Cragg."

The Mexican eyed him narrowly. "Why you not say so? But

42

I'm not know where he ees. Las' night I see heem; today he's gone."

"Thought you didn't know him?"

"The *señor* misonnerstan'. I'm say he's no frien' of Miguel Rosas."

"That *is* different. If you locate him, let me know. I'm Jim Lanier of the Box L."

Miguel's teeth flashed in a grim smile. "You tell the *Señor* Strongarm that and I betcha my boots he gets the beeg surprise."

"He'll get a surprise, all right," promised Raiford, and wheeled his horse.

He rode back through the little basin, once more carefully scouting the cabin. His search was no more successful than the first one had been; there was nobody in sight, nothing that could have made the noise he had heard. He finally continued on his way, putting the mystery aside. If it wasn't Squat who had made that thump he wasn't interested anyway.

He spent the rest of the day roaming among the hills, tightening his belt a notch in lieu of dinner, determined to find Squat if he was there to be found. He came across many little parks, some of which showed evidence of the recent presence of cattle. Apparently Miguel Rosas rotated his stock among these places, taking advantage of the pasture and occasional springs. Raiford was certain that cattle bearing other than Circle Cross brands were also rotated. Investigation by strangers would be anticipated by the watcher on the peak, and steps could be taken by the wily Rosas to secrete or rid himself of any cattle the possession of which might lead to embarrassment.

He gave up the search at the approach of dusk. He had no provisions or equipment for a prolonged search, and he did not want to remain away from the Box L any longer than was necessary. If the man whom Jake Rails had sent to Calixto to take James Lanier's place were to present himself to Newt Cragg during his absence, the lawyer would most certainly prepare a trap for him; and Raiford did not wish to lose either his freedom or his life before he had a chance to produce the real son. That was his one anchor, his only guaranty of good faith in assuming the masquerade—his ability to come forward with the man he had saved from an assassin's bullet the first night of this strange adventure.

He started back towards the Box L with the assurance that Squat was remaining out of circulation until the furore over Abe Ardell's death had subsided. Later, when he had shed his weariness, Raiford would return to the Circle Cross and, if he were lucky, surprise Squat. If it were at all possible he would take the man alive. There had been no witnesses to the shooting of Abe Ardell but himself; Squat must live in order to be forced to talk.

His horse was picking its way along the base of a section of rimrock that rose at Raiford's right, and though his mind was busy with his thoughts his eyes continued their methodical searching out of hiding places along the trail. Nevertheless, when the man appeared it was so suddenly, so unexpectedly that Raiford was momentarily paralyzed with surprise.

The horseman seemed to emerge from the bare face of the cliff not more than thirty feet away from Raiford and he was looking away from Joe when his horse stepped into sight. Then the sound of Raiford's approach reached him and his head swiveled and Joe looked squarely into the startled, ugly face of Squat Armstrong. The reactions of both men were immediate and instinctive; both snatched out their guns at the same time.

Both weapons snapped up and roared, and what might have been the result if Raiford's horse had not shied it is impossible to say. Raiford, having turned loose his own horse the night before, was riding an animal chosen at random from the Box L corral, and evidently the animal had not been broken to gunfire. The upward flash of Raiford's Colt alarmed it, and the horse leaped to the left as the men fired. Joe felt the tug of Squat's bullet as it tore through his right sleeve; Armstrong gave a yelp of pain and his gun went spinning out of his hand as the slug from Raiford's Colt ripped along the back of his hand. Disarmed, Squat wheeled his horse and disappeared into the side of the cliff.

Raiford was struggling with his frantic horse, and by the time he got it under control Squat had disappeared. Raiford spurred forward and understood at once how Armstrong had vanished. There was a narrow fissure in the rimrock wide enough for a horse to enter. He plunged in boldly, caution overcome by the desire to come to grips with Squat.

Once inside, the already fading light was completely shut off. Raiford pressed on as rapidly as he could safely do so, straining for a sight of Squat in the deep gloom. And quite suddenly his horse halted, throwing up its head, and refused to advance farther.

Swearing softly at the delay, Raiford slipped to the ground, ducked beneath the horse's head and felt his way forward. He stopped as abruptly as had the horse when he walked into a barrier of rock. The fissure had ended; they could not go ahead and there was not enough room to turn.

He backed his horse a step at a time and presently felt a breath of air on his face and discerned an opening in one side of the passage. He turned into this, and as the cleft widened he remounted and kept going. After a hundred yards or so he caught the grayness of twilight through an opening ahead and, dismounting, moved cautiously forward.

He reached the opening and had time for one sweeping glance. It was another of those parks into which he looked, but details were vague in the half-light. He had an impression of rock outcroppings and grass-green gullies; then a bullet smacked against the rocks close to his head and he hurriedly ducked back into the fissure.

Drawing his rifle from its boot, he crawled back to the entrance, his gaze fixed on the point from whence the shot had come. There was no movement, no sign of Squat or his horse; but there was plenty of cover for the man, and the animal could have been hidden behind one of the rock formations.

Narrowly Raiford scanned the terrain, then began working down the incline, using the brush at the side of the trail to screen him. Squat fired again and the bullet clipped leaves from the brush that shielded Joe. Instantly Joe came to his knees and flung two quick shots at the flash. Squat, he saw now, was crouched behind some rocks on the lip of a gully.

Raiford picked another clump of rocks as his objective and grimly made for it. By waddling like a duck on bent legs he was able to keep his rifle ready for a quick shot. He saw Armstrong's hat rise cautiously from his place of concealment and drove a bullet at it. Perhaps if he had not been so anxious to take the man alive he might not have missed.

He gained the rocks finally, but now darkness was falling rapidly and he knew he must get Squat within the next half hour or lose him entirely. He raised his head and drew a quick shot from the killer. Then he relaxed to think things over. After a moment he removed his hat and cautiously raised his eyes above the level of the rocks. He could see Squat's rifle resting on some rocks at the edge of the gully, but the man himself was out of sight.

The gully; if he could reach that he might sneak along its bed and take Squat from the rear. He mapped his course carefully; then, in order to hold Squat's attention, he placed his own rifle, pointed in Armstrong's direction, on the rocks. Then he drew his six-gun and started crawling through the brush.

No Indian moved more silently or cautiously. Occasionally he raised his head to scrutinize the rocks behind which Squat had taken refuge. The rifle was still there.

The half hour which he had allowed himself had expired when he rose to his feet, crouching, and moved forward, his eyes stabbing the gloom which surrounded him. He came to a short turn and knew that it was beyond this where Squat had holed up. He inched around it, his jaws locked with the fixity of his purpose. There must be no hesitation; a quick leap around the rock, a glance which must locate Squat instantly, then a quick

45

hard blow with the barrel of the gun squarely atop Squat's bullet-like head.

He waited an instant to coordinate mind and muscle, then leaped. And almost in the same instant he heard the boom of a six-gun on the other side of the basin.

He checked his violent action and lowered the upraised Colt with an oath of exasperation. Squat's rifle rested on the rocks where he had left it, but Squat himself was gone.

Raiford sprang to the top of the gully and peered across the basin. It was just light enough to show him Squat standing behind Raiford's hiding place, a smoking gun in his hand. If it hadn't been so disheartening it would have been comical. While Raiford was circling to the east to flank Squat, Squat had circled to the west to flank Raiford.

Joe raised his gun and fired as rapidly as he could draw the hammer, but he fired in futile anger more than with any hope of hitting the man. And Squat, snatching up Raiford's rifle, made straight up the trail towards the fissure where Joe had left his horse.

To follow on foot would have been foolish; Joe got Squat's rifle and after a short search found his horse. Almost recklessly he ascended the path to the fissure and entered the cleft, for now the darkness was so deep that a shot from Squat was but a remote possibility. He found his way to the main road, knew that he had lost his man, and headed for the Box L.

It was very late when he reached the house, but Pop Lanier was still in his chair on the gallery.

"I've been ramming around in the hills." Raiford was angered by his failure to capture Squat and his manner was short. "You can't tell me it's the Double A stealing your stock; it's Miguel Rosas."

"You're crazy."

"Yeah? Well, I'll eat raw and without salt all the beef the Double A has stolen. Pop, you're being played for a sucker and you haven't the sense to realize it."

"Is that so! You're tryin' to tell me I'm dumb as well as blind, huh? Well, maybe you can tell me who's playin' me for a sucker."

"Sure I can tell you. It's Newt Cragg. For Pete's sake, don't go spilling the news to him until I can pin it on him."

He stamped into the house and hunted up something for them to eat.

7

ABE ARDELL was buried the next day. They laid him to rest on a high fenced-in knoll beside the son who had died in infancy.

Everybody of importance in Calixto attended the funeral, and out of respect for him the business places in town were closed until noon. Newt Cragg was there, quietly sympathetic and comforting. It was Newt who walked between Alice and Mrs. Ardell, supporting them in their grief by his gentle words and touch. When it was over, Alice lingered a moment to thank him.

"I don't know what we'd have done without you, Newt. You've been fine. I can't thank you too much."

He smiled gently. "Abe was my friend, and I have always hoped that in time the relationship would become even closer." There was no mistaking his meaning and a soft blush crept into the girl's pale cheeks and she lowered her eyes. Newt went on. "It is I who should be thankful for the opportunity to show my affection to some small extent. I'd ask nothing better than the privilege of doing things for you the rest of our lives; as it is, if there is anything—"

"Thanks, Newt. I'll not forget."

He took her hand and held it between both his own. "Above all, don't brood. I'll ride over occasionally; you need diversion —something to take your mind off things."

"Please do," she said earnestly. "As often as you can."

At that moment she was as close to loving Newt Cragg as she was ever to be.

Joe Raiford watched the funeral from the top of a ridge on the Box L. He couldn't see very much, just the little clump of figures that moved slowly to the burial place and stood in silence while the service was being read. He watched it squatted on his heels and smoking a cigarette. He wished he could be there to offer Alice what comfort he could, but that wasn't possible. His presence would only disturb her more, feeling as she must that he or his men were responsible for Abe's death. When it was over, he got up, ground out the cigarette stub and climbed onto his horse.

He sat there for a moment thinking. The pieces of the puzzle were beginning to fit into a symmetrical pattern. His first theory—that Miguel Rosas was entirely responsible for the rustling for his own profit—was out, for the Box L undoubtedly knew where their cattle were going.

The second theory, that Newt Cragg had a financial interest in the Circle Cross and was engineering the rustling to enrich himself, did not explain the presence of a son on Pop Lanier's ranch. Unless—Raiford's eyes narrowed in concentration—unless he had been fetched in to cover up, to give orders, to hide the truth from Pop. Any losses that Pop might become aware of would cause him to fume and fuss, but certainly he would not blame his own son for them. Or would he? Was the fake son to be the goat? Would he, after the ranch had been stripped, have a furious quarrel with the old man and once more depart in anger? Could be. But somehow the theory rang no bull's eye bell in Raiford's mind.

The third theory remained and Raiford was inclined to accept it. In some manner Newt Cragg planned to use the son to obtain possession of the Box L. If he were to marry Alice Ardell, he'd have a strangle hold on the Double A also. In fact, if he were to marry her now, he'd practically own the ranch. It would be the property of Abe's widow, of course; but the management of it would be in Alice's hands—or her husband's. From struggling cow-town lawyer to wealthy cattleman was a huge stride. Things were shaping up nicely for Newton Cragg. And he, Montana Joe Raiford, was the only one with the knowledge or the incentive to spoil the beautiful plan.

He had a theory—and the real James Lanier. There was no proof to back the theory, and if he produced young Lanier at this time Newt would protest that he had been honestly deceived. Nothing to gain that way. The only concrete thing with which he had to work was the certain knowledge that it was Squat Armstrong who had shot Ardell. He must capture Squat and he must do it without help, for nobody seemed to know the man except his evil associates; and Raiford's story of the killing would not be accepted without question. And he wasn't in a position to answer questions.

His helplessness stirred a sullen anger within him which fanned into flame when he returned to the Box L. Since his arrival no ranch work whatever had been attempted. Trotter had been hired merely to facilitate the rustling; he was not interested in the ranch and took advantage of his employer's blindness to shirk. Well, thought Raiford, if I'm accepted as Lanier's son I'll play the part to the full. He sharply ordered the lounging cowboys to saddle up and prepare to haze stock down from the hills.

Trotter got off the bench, glowering. He appeared even bigger and more brutal than ever as he growled, "Who the hell you givin' orders to?"

"You. If you don't like it, get your time."

"I was hired by Newt Cragg."

"What did he hire you for—to sit around on your tail?"

The question was embarrassing, inasmuch as Trotter couldn't very well explain to James Lanier that he'd been hired to make trouble. He gave Raiford a venomous look and turned towards the corral.

Raiford led his horse down to the inclosure and stood waiting for them to saddle up, and presently the man named Hurd came out with his horse and started rigging it.

Hurd said in a low voice, "You want to watch that jigger.

He's buildin' up a head of steam and he's gonna pop pretty soon."

"Let him pop. Hurd, how come you signed on with this outfit?"

"Just happened to drift into town and met up with Trotter at the Royal Flush. He was lookin' for hands and I was lookin' for a job."

"You didn't know what kind of a job it was?"

"I thought it was cow nussin'."

"What was it?"

"Cow nussin'—partly. Once in a while we'd gather a bunch and shove 'em into one of the toppin'-off pastures."

"And shortly afterwards they'd be rustled. Ever wonder about it?"

"I was bein' paid for helpin' to put them there, and not for wonderin' what became of 'em afterwards."

He jerked the latigo tight and swung into his saddle. He had told Raiford all he intended to tell.

They spent the rest of the day hazing stock out of the east hills, returning at sundown. Pop greeted him with a complaint.

"Always leave somebody around here to saddle up for me. Don't you think I get tired of settin' in this danged chair? Go down and throw my hull on that bay; I'm goin' for a ride. I'll eat when I come back."

"It's beginning to get dark."

"Don't mean nothin' to me," said Pop bitterly. "I'm always in the dark."

Raiford saddled up for him and put the rein into his hand. Lanier got into the saddle and sent the bay trotting out of the yard. Raiford found himself wondering what would happen to Pop if his horse stepped into a hole and broke a leg. Lanier might wander about the range until he fell into a ravine and broke his neck, or he might starve to death before they could find him. Yet he could not blame the old man; riding was the only means he had of lightening the monotony of eternal darkness.

If he were to meet with an accident, thought Raiford, nobody would miss him very much. He was certainly the meanest old man Joe had ever met. He had no interest in what his son had done for twelve years, no desire to recall the past, no question to ask about his dead wife. From Raiford's viewpoint it was a fortunate thing that Pop was so indifferent; a few well-put questions would reveal to Lanier that Joe was not his son.

Lanier did not take a long ride; Raiford had just finished his supper when he saw the bay come ambling into the yard and stop before the feed shed. Joe went out and headed Lanier for the house, then put up and fed the horse. Pop was eating supper when he returned to the house.

"What's that you was tellin' me about Newt's playin' me for a sucker?" he asked Raiford.

"You'd better forget that until I have more to go on. I just can't see the Double A rustling our stock, that's all. I think it's Miguel Rosas and his outfit. I think they run our stuff over the Double A to cover their trail. I found out today that the rustling takes place right after your crew of cutthroats round up some prime beef and put it in a pasture that's convenient for the rustlers to get at."

"What's that got to do with Newt?"

"He hired the crew, didn't he?"

Pop stared at him with his sightless eyes, his fork suspended just outside his mouth. Deliberately he put down the fork. "Why, the damned double-crossin' so-and-so!"

"Probably. But don't go calling him that to his face until I give you the word."

"You figger he's workin' with Rosas?"

"I don't know, but I aim to find out. That's why I don't want you to say anything to Newt yet. He's smart, and if he knows you suspect him he'll cover up. By the way, today's the end of the month. Do you pay the men off or does Cragg?"

Pop growled an oath. "How can I when I can't see to count the money? Newt pays 'em. By grab, if he's stealin' my cattle he's stealin' my money too! Boy, if you get the goods on him I'll take him apart piece by piece, eyes or no eyes."

"You can have the job. Just hang onto that temper of yours until we know for sure."

When he'd cleaned up the dishes and gone out onto the gallery where Pop was sitting he saw that the men were saddling up. He walked down among them and Hurd said, "You payin' off? Or do we collect from Cragg same as usual?"

"Cragg'll pay you this time. We'll probably have other arrangements by the end of next month. All the men riding to Calixto?"

"Everybody includin' the cook. Payday only comes once a month."

"Watch your step, Hurd. They buried Abe Ardell today and the Double A is on the prod. If the two outfits meet there may be trouble."

Hurd nodded and stepped into his saddle and the crew rode away in a bunch. Raiford stood there considering as the dusk swallowed them, then caught up Squat's horse and put Armstrong's rig on it. His own mount was roaming the range, having been turned loose by Raiford on the night Ardell was shot, and the Box L horse he had ridden into the hills had been appropriated by Squat when he made his escape from the basin.

Raiford rode to the gallery and stopped to speak to Pop. "I'm going to Calixto. Folks think we're responsible for

Ardell's death and there might be trouble. Are you going to be all right out here alone?"

"Of course I'll be all right. What you think I am—a baby?"

Raiford followed the crew to Calixto. He saw the Box L horses standing outside Newt Cragg's office and knew they were inside getting their pay. Farther down the street and on the opposite side more horses stood at the hitching rail of the Royal Flush and he guessed that the Double A men were inside the saloon. He tied up in front of the store and walked to a little building with the words MARSHAL'S OFFICE painted on its window. There was a light inside and the door was open. He entered and saw a short, stout man with a badge pinned onto his vest.

Raiford said, "I guess you're the marshal. I'm Jim Lanier. My men are in town and I reckon the Double A boys are, too. Better keep your eyes open for trouble."

The marshal gave him a mean look. "If your fellers start anything I'll sure enough have 'em open wide. If the Double A gets the jump on them, I'll be as blind as Pop Lanier himself."

"You're a hell of a lawman," said Raiford disgustedly, and walked out.

He went to the Royal Flush and leaned against the wall, watching Newt's office on the other side of the street. Presently Trotter and the men came trooping out and headed in a compact bunch for the Royal Flush. When they reached the sidewalk Raiford intercepted them.

"Not in here, boys. Not tonight."

"Who says so?" Trotter wanted to know.

"I do."

"By jacks, this is a public place; we got as much right in it as that crowd from the Double A."

"You can find other places where the liquor is just as good. If you go in there you'll just be asking for trouble. The whole town's down on us and the marshal is backing the Double A. Spend your money somewhere else."

"And tell the whole stinkin' town we're scared of Thorne's outfit!"

Raiford lost his patience. "Damn you. Trotter, I'm not going to stand here and argue with you! I'm ordering you to stay out of the Royal Flush; if you want a fight, come back in the alley and I'll try to accommodate you."

"Feller, there ain't nothin' I'd like better!"

Hurd spoke up. "Don't be a bigger fool than nature made you, Trotter. Jim's plumb right. We'd be crazy to walk in there right after they've buried Ardell. If anything started we'd have the whole town to lick. Come on, let's go to the Silver Saddle and bust the faro bank." He took the nearest man by the arm and started up the street with him; and the others, after a little hesitation, followed, leaving Raiford and Trotter glaring at each other.

"You still feel like takin' me back in the alley?" grated Trotter.

"Not unless you insist. I'm even going to back water. I'm going to tell you that if you want to go into the Royal Flush alone, you can go ahead."

"Think I'm plumb crazy?" Trotter sent a venomous glare after the men trooping along the dark sidewalk. "Danged yella-bellies! And that feller Hurd; I'll fix his clock for him one of these days."

He turned and slouched along the walk, growling to himself.

Raiford went into the shadow of the wall and waited there, determined to stand guard until the Double A crew left the place. The sounds inside were subdued and he guessed that the cowboys were restraining themselves out of respect for their dead boss. That restraint would snap at the appearance of a Box L man for there wasn't one on the Double A crew who didn't believe that Ardell had been shot by one of the Lanier outfit.

The light in Newt Cragg's office went out, then Newt came from the building and cut across the street towards the Royal Flush. He halted on the sidewalk and looked about him. He saw Raiford's shape against the wall and came towards him, peering.

"It's me," Raiford told him.

"Oh! Jim. Where are the boys?"

"Down at the Silver Saddle. I talked them out of the Royal Flush."

"Good idea. They'd be massacred, and cowhands are hard to get. Sure they won't come back?"

"They might. But they won't go inside. I aim to park right here until Thorne and his men pull out."

"You'll probably have a long wait. Well, I'm going in and have a quick one, then turn in. Had a long ride out in the country to fix up some papers and I'm dead on my feet."

He pushed through the swinging doors and into the saloon. In a few minutes he emerged and started across the street without even glancing at Raiford. Raiford saw the light go on in the office, then slowly die as Cragg carried the lamp into a rear room. For a few minutes he saw a side window glow dully, then go dark. Newt had evidently retired.

Raiford's wait was not as long as Newt Cragg had predicted. He smoked cigarettes and alternately squatted on his heels or leaned against the wall. Men passed in and out of the place, but there were no Box L cowboys among them. An hour passed. Then he heard Mel Thorne's voice saying, "Well, come on, boys; this is one payday we're pullin' out early," and the whole Double A crew came out to the street. They were quiet and orderly as they climbed onto their horses and headed homeward.

Raiford stretched and gave a sigh of relief. No need for him to remain on guard any longer. He walked slowly down to the store and got onto his own horse and rode slowly after them. The night was quiet and balmy and he held his horse to a walk, having no desire to catch up with the Double A men. His problem ever with him, he found himself wondering why the fake James Lanier sent down by Jake Rails had not yet made his appearance. Perhaps the right man had been harder to find than Newt Cragg had anticipated.

He was conscious at first of the roll of hoofs ahead of him but even after these sounds had died in the distance he held to a slow pace. It was not late and he was in no hurry to reach the Box L. His horse halted and he suddenly realized that he had reached the fork in the trail. He reined the animal to the left and as he did so glanced towards the place where he had first sighted the Box L buildings. Then he jerked the horse to an abrupt halt and stared. There was a ruddy glow in the sky to the southeast that could mean only one thing: a fire.

He swore worriedly and spurred his horse to a gallop. Pop would have gone to bed long before this; if the house was afire the blind old man was in grave danger.

The glow brightened with startling suddenness and a shower of sparks erupted into the air. Then came a huge burst of flame and by its light Raiford saw that it was indeed the house which was burning. He swore again and urged his horse to an even faster pace.

Progress seemed agonizingly slow, and the flames were roaring when he finally rode into the yard. Because of the heat he was forced to halt near the corral. Inside the inclosure the horses were milling about, snorting their fright. He tied his mount securely and circled the building yelling, "Pop! Pop! Where are you?"

There was no answer, and the sickening conviction reached him that the blind old man was surely inside that inferno. The heat was increasing and he could not reach Pop's room without some protection against it. He dashed into the bunkhouse and snatched up a couple of blankets. He soaked them in the watering trough and draped one about him. The other he carried in his arms.

The front wall was smoking but it had not yet burst into flame. He ran up onto the gallery, found the door and burst through it into the living room. The smoke was thick, but he found the door to Pop's room. He yanked at it. It refused to open. He called Pop's name again and got no answer. He ran outside and circled the building, his blanket steaming.

Gasping and choking, he reached the window of Pop's room;

53

then, despite the heat, he halted to stare. Vertically across the window, from top to sill, a wide board had been nailed with heavy spikes. Even if Pop had succeeded in opening the window he could not have escaped. Raiford swore harshly and ran to the blacksmith shop. He believed now that the door had been nailed shut also.

He found a crowbar and returned to the house. Even with this heavy implement he had to exert all his strength to pry loose the heavy nails. He threw the board aside and retreated to get a breath of fresh air; but before he left he saw that the window was open wide.

He drew the blanket about him and once more advanced to the window. Draping the second blanket over the sill, he leaped upward and forward and hung suspended over the sill, half in and half out of the room. And directly beneath him lay Pop Lanier, sprawled face down on the floor.

Raiford draped the second wet blanket over his body and, despite the heat which seared his bare hands, got hold of Pop's extended arms. He heaved, panting and choking, and got the slight form to the level of the sill. He kicked free and dropped back to the ground, heaving and dragging. With a last desperate effort he got the old man's head and shoulders through the window, then pulled with all his strength. Pop came through and Raiford went down with the unconscious man atop him. He struggled up and ran, dragging Lanier after him.

Back on the cool grass he let go and dropped down beside the old man. He gulped in great gusts of clean air, found his scarf with blistered hands and sponged the tears from his burning eyes. And at last he was in a condition to examine Pop.

Lanier was not dead. He had pulled his trousers over a nightshirt and had put on his boots. Cloth and leather were scorched and Pop's shock of gray hair was singed; but he still lived and breathed. He had been overcome by smoke and, falling to the floor, had escaped some of the effects of the intense heat.

Raiford worked on him, raising and lowering his arms rhythmically to pump fresh air into his lungs, and finally Pop groaned and opened his sightless eyes. Raiford said, "You're all right now, Pop. Take it easy," and ran for the mess shack. He scooped up a cupful of lard and ran back to Pop and spread it liberally over the old man's burns. Then he applied the same remedy to his blistered hands.

After a while Pop was able to sit up and talk, and the story he told in a shaken voice was a horrible one. He had been awakened by the sound of pounding and had immediately smelled smoke and, he thought, kerosene. He thought somebody was trying to arouse him and, putting on trousers and boots, found his way to the door. He could not open it. Then had come a pounding from the direction of the window, and when he groped his way to that and finally got it open, it was to find a plank nailed across the opening. He knew then that he had been deliberately penned in the burning house. He found his gun and fired through the window, but not being able to see had no means of knowing what effect his shots had had.

Then had come the crackling of flames and the beginning of the intense heat. Smoke was filling the room and Pop became frantic. He stumbled about trying to find an exit which did not exist, hurling his slight form against the heavy door which refused to budge. Exhaustion speeded the end. He had fallen unconscious as he was trying to grope his way to the window.

Raiford forgot the pain of his burns in the red rage which consumed him. Pop was a mean old man and the world undoubtedly would be better off without him; but this horrible crime stirred Raiford as he had rarely been stirred before.

His thoughts flew at once to Newt Cragg. Abe Ardell's death had been a fortunate accident as far as the lawyer was concerned; it was too much to believe that a second accident, equally fortunate, should follow the first so closely. Yet Newt had gone to bed in Calixto two hours before. Or had he?

By the time the Box L crew returned from town, the house had been reduced to smoking, smoldering ashes.

8

THERE WAS a fairly substantial shed which had been used for storage, and Raiford and Pop Lanier bedded down in it, using blankets borrowed from members of the crew.

Joe's burns were confined to his hands and were superficial though painful. Pop was pretty well baked, but he was three-fourths mummy anyway and would be as well as ever in a few days. It was the rather cynical opinion of most of the men that Pop had merely had a preview of what was in store for him when he finally did cash in his chips, and Raiford was inclined to agree with them.

He knew now that his third theory was the correct one. Everything fitted. Although there was no means of proving that Newt had set the fire, he was as certain of the lawyer's guilt as though Newt had given him a written confession. The reason for the presence of James Lanier was now apparent. As the son of Pop Lanier, the ranch would be his upon Pop's death. Newt had intended hastening Pop's end and would immediately "buy" the ranch from the fake son. He would then secure the Double A by marrying Alice.

Raiford knew now that Newt had not retired after their conversation in front of the Royal Flush. Knowing that everybody but Pop had left the Box L and feeling certain that Raiford would be forced to remain on guard before the saloon until long after midnight, Newt had gone out the back way, had got his horse from the stable and had ridden to the Box L for the purpose of firing the house.

Newt had done the thing himself. He was far too crafty to trust another, even such a callous person as Squat Armstrong. Nailing the old man in so that he could not possibly escape was a perfectly sound procedure, for the destruction of the house would mean the destruction of the evidence that he had been trapped by man-made means; it would be assumed that the smoke had overcome him while he slept. And this plan would have succeeded but for the fact that the Double A crew had left Calixto prematurely and as a consequence Raiford had returned ahead of the schedule Newt had set.

It was a callous, coldblooded crime, and Raiford seethed in impotent anger at his inability to pin it where it belonged. Even if he should find somebody who had seen Newt leave town it would be impossible to prove that he had set the fire unless there had been a witness to the actual deed; and there had been nobody on the Box L or within miles of it but the blind man. If Lanier believed that Newt had set it, he was vindictive enough to swear that he had recognized Newt by his voice; but Pop had already told Raiford that he had heard no sound from the person except the hammering as the nails were driven home, and Raiford would not be satisfied with perjured evidence. For this reason he decided not to allow Newt Cragg to be brought forward as a suspect.

"It was somebody from the Double A," declared Pop bitterly. "That Thorne feller, maybe. Figgered he was gettin' even for your shootin' of Abe Ardell. But you outfoxed 'em, boy. Now we got all the excuse we need for rubbin' 'em out. Ride over there with the whole crew and clean 'em up!"

"We can't do that with the little we have to go on. I rode out right behind Thorne and his men; none of them would have had time to get that fire going and nail you in before I got here."

"You said Newt aimed to make a sucker of me; mebbe he's aimin' to make me a corpse likewise. Where was he?" The blind eyes were expressionless, but every other feature of the old man registered suspicion and distrust.

"Newt seems to be in the clear. He was in town and paid off the crew. I saw him in the Royal Flush before I left Calixto." Which, while being the truth, was far from being the whole truth.

"Well, what you goin' to do about it? You want to give the orders; get busy and give some."

"The only order I aim to give right now is that somebody must stay on the spread with you night and day no matter what happens."

They ate breakfast with the crew the next morning, and when the meal was finished Raiford directed the removal of the trash from the shed and its cleaning and repairing. There was a loft overhead with a three-foot-square opening, but the ladder which gave access to it had long since been removed and Raiford did not bother to disturb its contents. Two bunks were built, another window was cut in the wall, and the cook stove, now burned brown, was fished from the ashes and set up. A rough table and two chairs were built, and boxes were nailed to the wall to form a cupboard of sorts. After dinner, Raiford set them to building a roofed porch for Pop's use, then set out in search of the horse he had turned loose. He had no wish to use Squat's pony, and the others on the Box L that were available might prove gun-shy.

He rode aimlessly, taking a meandering course across the range until he came to the hills on the western side of the valley. He had not seen a sign of his horse, so he started up a path which led into the hills and after several minutes of gentle ascent caught sight of a saddled horse tethered to a tree. He approached it cautiously, finally dropping to the ground and leading his mount. And thus he came unexpectedly upon Alice Ardell.

She was sitting on a rock where she could gaze out over the valley, her chin in her hands, her eyes brooding. She did not turn her head at his approach, but he knew that she must have seen him crossing the valley and could have avoided him had she wished to.

"Good afternoon," he said quietly. She did not answer and he dropped the rein and walked over to her. "Mind if I sit down?"

Still she did not answer, and he seated himself beside her. For a few moments there was silence, but he saw her gaze slant towards his bandaged hands.

She said, "I suppose you think it was the Double A who set the fire."

"So you knew there was a fire."

"The boys saw the glow in the sky." Her voice was flat, dead. "Under the circumstances they did nothing about it. They didn't report it to me until this morning. If they had, I'm not sure that I would have done anything about it either." There was another short pause; then, "Was anybody—hurt?"

"No. I followed the Double A men from town and got Pop out in time."

He caught the little sigh of relief and went on. "As for the Double A doing it, I'm quite sure they didn't."

57

"They had every reason to—or thought they had."

He too was gazing out over the range. He said, "When I first met you that day in Calixto you said that things were all wrong but that you were sure we could find a solution to our troubles and misunderstandings. Since then I've been trying hard to justify your faith. I've learned some things that you should know.

"The rustling, for instance. Pop Lanier believes that you are stealing his stock; you believe that it is being planted on your spread to make trouble. You're both partly right and partly wrong. The Box L stock is being rustled and it's being run across the Double A. But the one who is doing it is Miguel Rosas of the Circle Cross."

"Rosas?" She was looking at him now. "Why should he run them across the Double A?"

"To cover the trail, maybe. Maybe for a deeper reason. At any rate it's Miguel's men who are doing the rustling. I know that. That's why I could assure you that none of the Box L men had a hand in the drive that resulted in your father's death."

"Jim, what are you telling me!"

"I'm telling you that the two spreads are at each other's throats because of misunderstanding, misrepresentation and some very skillful dirty work. I suppose Mel Thorne told you that he found every man of ours in the bunkhouse fast asleep that night."

"Yes," she answered slowly. "Yes, he did. He couldn't understand it, and it made him mad. He believed that your men did it, especially since he chased somebody over the Box L range."

Raiford smiled grimly. "If it had been a Box L man, I think our range would be the last place he'd head for. He certainly wouldn't want to advertise the fact that he was from the Box L."

"You mean that the man who shot father was one of Rosas' Mexicans."

"Not necessarily a Mexican; but it was somebody with them."

He hesitated for a moment, debating just how much he could tell her. Newt Cragg must not be brought in at this point; he had no definite proof that he could give her without revealing his false identity. She had known Newt a long time and liked him; she would not take the word of a confessed impostor that Newt was at the bottom of such a vile and complicated plot.

He said, "Listen, Alice. Before I came down here I was a marshal in a Montana gold town. I caught a killer named Squat Armstrong and had him convicted and sentenced to hang. He escaped and swore to get even with me. Yesterday while I was prowling around the Circle Cross I ran into him. He got away from me, but I'm sure that he was helping to drive those cattle and that he killed your father."

She got to her feet, her body taut. "Why didn't you say so at once? This man must be caught and punished. I'll send my crew up to the Circle Cross at once. If we find a single stolen animal we'll settle this rustling business once and for all."

He reached up and put a restraining hand on her arm. "We can't do that just yet, Alice. Sit down and I'll tell you why."

She hesitated for a moment, then slowly resumed her seat.

He said, "I went up there yesterday for the same purpose—to find Squat and choke the truth from him, and to look for rustled cattle. Long before I reached the Circle Cross I caught the flash of field glasses from the top of a ridge and knew I was being watched. There are dozens of little parks up there, many of them with hidden entrances. The stolen stuff is probably kept together and they'd have time to move them before we got there. I didn't find a single stolen animal, but many of those parks had been recently occupied. I ran into Squat by accident, and we had a long-range battle. After my barging in, they'll cover up and be very careful for a while."

"But what are we going to do? We can't just sit down and let them get away with it."

"It's something that must be handled very carefully. We can't make a move until we know exactly where we're going. I've been trained to find things out; I want you to leave it all to me for the time being. After all, it's the Box L that's under a cloud, myself in particular; can't you see how anxious I am to find Squat Armstrong and prove that he shot your father? I've got to do that. But I've got to do it in my own way."

She looked steadily at him for a time, then said, "All right, Jim; I'll leave it to you. I've never been able to convince myself that you were guilty of—of anything. Your men, yes; they're a hard bunch. You know that. You saw how Trotter tried to force a fight on Mel there at Calixto." She made a swift gesture. "Why do you keep them, Jim? Why don't you fire those gunmen and hire real cowboys?"

He smiled at her. "You've got to remember one thing: this whole show is being managed by someone very sharp and very clever. There's a reason for every move that has been made in the past and that is to be made in the future. I don't want to spoil his setup; I'm beginning to see his plan, and if I change things he may alter it and I'd have to start all over again. You've got to keep mum about what I've told you. I want you to promise that you will. Don't mention it to a soul except, possibly, your mother. And trust me, Alice. I've just got to have your faith and your confidence. Will you give me your promise?"

Her eyes met his, looked beyond them and into the mind and

59

soul of him. She drew a deep breath and nodded her head. "Yes. I'm going to trust you, Jim. And I'm not going to tell a soul."

He extended his hand impulsively and she solemnly took it. For a short while they sat there, gazes locked; then she withdrew her fingers and got up. There was color in her cheeks now.

"I've got to go. But come over to see us, Jim. I want the boys to know that I believe in you. It will help a lot."

He shook his head as he rose. "I'm afraid not, Alice. As long as they don't know what you and I know they must suspect the Box L. It's better that way. It's the way this—person —wants it. It would be even better if you'd continue to pretend that you distrust me. You understand, don't you?"

"Not entirely, Jim. You say that the thing is much deeper than plain rustling, that the person is sharp and very clever. Who is it? And what is his plan?"

"I wish I could tell you, but I can't. Not yet, Alice. I'm morally certain of the plan and the man, but I haven't any real proof. Until I get it I'm not going to accuse anybody except in my own mind. When I'm absolutely sure, I'll tell you."

She had to be satisfied with that. He helped her to mount, watched as she picked her way down the trail and headed for the Double A; then he rode down onto the range and set out towards the Box L. When he rode into the yard he saw that the porch had been finished and that Pop was seated in a chair with a rawhide seat which had been fashioned to his order. The men were lounging around the bunkhouse and although it was not quitting time Raiford decided to let them lounge. They had worked well that day.

As he was off-saddling, Hurd rode up with a spare horse at the end of his rope. He said to Raiford, "This is your hoss, ain't it? Found him over at that spring near the east hills."

"Yes, he's mine. I was out looking for him myself. Got away from me a couple of days ago."

Hurd nodded, his eyes narrowing. "Lost him the night Abe Ardell got shot, didn't you?"

"I did." He studied Hurd for a moment. The man was hard, but he was square. "Fact is, I turned him loose that night. It was me the Double A chased. But I didn't shoot Abe Ardell."

His eyes did not falter under Hurd's hard stare, and finally Hurd said, "I'm glad you told me that. You coulda lied about it."

Raiford took the horse from him and put it into the corral. He said to Hurd, "Much obliged," and the thanks were not merely for the finding of the horse. The trust and confidence of a man like this was something to be thankful for.

Trotter rode to Calixto immediately after supper. He saw a light in Newt Cragg's office and entered without knocking. Newt was behind his desk, and for a moment Trotter stood, big and belligerent, in the doorway; then he strode up to the desk and looked through the yellow lamplight at the calm-eyed lawyer.

Newt said, "Yes?"

"I want my time."

"You got it yesterday, Trot. You've only one day coming."

"I'm talkin' about the bonus you promised me. I've done everything you told me to do. Rosas has always found the stuff right where he was supposed to, right age, right number—everything. I've tried to nail Mel Thorne's hide to the barn, and the only thing that stopped me from doin' it was this Lanier feller hornin' in. Now I'm through."

"Why?"

"Because I ain't takin' no more orders from Lanier. I didn't sign on to work cows or build fences and shacks. I ain't standin' for it no longer."

"So Mr. Jim Lanier is proving a bit objectionable, eh?" Newt's eyes glinted and his jaws clicked shut. "I find him so myself. I can't blame you for not liking to take his orders, Trot, but for the moment it's necessary that you do. Stick it out for another week and I'll add a hundred to that bonus. How does that sound to you?"

It sounded pretty good, and some of the stubborn anger in Trotter's face changed to avarice.

"I don't like it, but a hundred bucks is a hundred bucks. But, by grab! I ain't stayin' no more'n a week. That's flat, Newt."

"A week will be time enough. Now how about that fire last night?"

"Who told you about it?"

"The Double A men saw it on their way home. What happened?"

"I don't rightly know. It was over when we got there. Jim Lanier rode back when the Double A left the Royal Flush. He got there in time to fish Pop out. If it was me I'da let him roast, the old buzzard!"

"How'd he happen to get caught? He can't see, but he knows his way around the house."

"I dunno. Passed out before he could get movin', I reckon. All Jim said was that he found him unconscious and drug him through the window."

"That's all he said?" Newt's sharp eyes drilled the man.

"What else was there to say?"

There was no doubting Trotter's ignorance of the nailed door and window; he was not subtle enough to hide his knowledge had he possessed any. That meant that the fake James Lanier was playing it foxy, and Newt thought he knew the reason. When the showdown came the fellow would use his knowledge as a weapon to demand more than the $500 due him. Newt's lips tightened under his neat mustache. He had already planned for just such a contingency.

He said, "Well, it's settled then. Hang on for another week and you get six hundred instead of five. Right?"

"Yeah. But no more'n a week."

He went out and Newt settled back in his chair, closed his eyes and proceeded to meditate. He indulged in some heavy mental damning, the damning being directed at the fake James Lanier. But for him this neat little plan of his would be well on its way to a favorable conclusion; Pop Lanier would have been out of the way, for which fact many people would be extremely grateful, and negotiations for the purchase of the Box L would have been concluded. So also would be the career of the fake James Lanier. As for the Double A—well, Alice had been very nice to him. The funeral had turned the tide in his favor. The supposed James Lanier no longer flourished as a rival. Abe Ardell's death, while somewhat premature, had occurred at a most favorable time for Newton Cragg.

Who had killed him—the fake James Lanier? Had he intercepted the drive and found himself in a position where he must shoot or be shot? Quite probable. On the other hand—

Newt's eyes popped open at the sound of a furtive knock, not on the front door but at the rear. Newt went quickly into the back room, closing the office door behind him and shutting out the light. He unbarred the back door and opened it and Squat Armstrong slipped through the entrance. Newt closed the door again.

"It's about time you showed up," he said coldly. "I've been waiting for a report from you."

Squat's voice was tense. "I been wantin' to see you bad enough. I started for Calixto and run into somebody I never expected to see in this neck of the woods."

"Yes? Who was it?"

"Marshal from up north. Montana Joe, they call him."

Newt was astonished. "What's he doing down here—got something on you?"

"Just a little matter of a killin' or two."

"I see. And you've been hiding from him."

"Hidin', hell! I've been *lookin'* for him. Had him dead to rights, but his hoss shied. His bullet scraped my fist and I dropped my gun and hada run for it. Had another under my arm but no chance to yank it. But now that I know he's here I'll shore git him next time. But, Newt, they's one thing I can't figger out. In the mix-up we swapped hosses and his is wearin' a Box L brand!"

Newt started in the darkness. "A Box L? Where'd he get it?"

"I dunno. Mebbe his own played out and he roped one on the Box L range. They got some runnin' loose."

Newt was worried. "That must be it. I'm mighty sure nobody on the Box L is a representative of the law. What happened on that last drive?"

Squat swore. "The Double A jumped us right after we'd crossed the crick. Somebody barged into me and I hada shoot him. Found out afterwards that it was Abe Ardell. His number turned up before it was due."

"That part of it's all right as long as nobody saw you shoot him."

"That's the hell of it. Somebody did. And he wasn't one of Rosas' boys. There was five of us drivin'. Miguel was at point and two of his crew ridin' swing. Me and that feller called Felipe had the drag. I seen Miguel and the two swing men cross the ridge. One of 'em got plugged in the arm. I left Miguel behind me when I started up the hill and barged into this other feller just before Ardell charged us. He went down and I cut for it. But he saw me plug Ardell, and I didn't figger out until later that he was an extry. I got me a hunch it was that Montana Joe."

"What would he be doing in a cattle drive?"

"Lookin' for me."

Newt thought it out in the darkness and finally said, "I wouldn't worry about it too much. You're out to get this lawman; well, get him and there'll be nobody to pin Ardell's killing on you. But watch your step; I'm going to need you and you won't be any good to me if you're dead."

"Don't you worry about me. Any new orders?"

"No. The cattle drives are over. Just keep in touch with Miguel so I can locate you in a hurry."

"I don't trust that Spick; he'd double-cross his own mother. And he acts like he's about ten times as good as me."

"Then keep your eye on him. If he gets too brash, you know what to do."

"You're danged tootin' I do! But I wanted to hear you tell me so."

He left and Newt returned to the office and some more meditation. The thing was shaping up magnificently. Eventually Miguel must be done away with; his usefulness was at an end. It wouldn't matter one bit if Armstrong shot him the very next day.

Pop Lanier must be eliminated, but not just now. Say within a week. A second accident following so closely upon the first might arouse suspicion. And he must wait for the opportunity. Then must come the fake son, Miguel, and Squat. He would use Squat to rid him of Lanier and the Mexican; he would attend to Squat himself. The man was a convicted killer and his death at Newt's hand would bring praise rather than condemnation.

DURING THE NEXT FEW DAYS, Raiford kept the crew busy despite the grumbling of Trotter. Cattle were hazed down to the range, fences were put in repair and equipment was overhauled. None of the men complained openly but Trotter, and Hurd seemed to take delight in seeing the big foreman forced to exert his strength on some task assigned him by Raiford. Hurd's amusement only angered Trotter the more, and it became plain that trouble between the two was to be expected at any moment.

Towards the end of the week Raiford decided that the time was ripe for another visit to the Circle Cross. If Squat had gone into hiding, the failure of the Montana lawman to show up again should have dispelled his fears, and his hand wound had probably healed to the extent that he could once more handle a six-gun with his accustomed dexterity.

He determined this time to make a day of it, and went to the corral immediately after breakfast. Trotter came out of the mess shack and joined him there.

"What is it today?" growled the foreman. "More fence stringin'?"

"You guessed it. The southwest pasture. Take the cook and the chuck wagon so the men won't have to come in at noon. I'm going to be away all day on business. I don't want Pop left alone for a minute. Tell Hurd to stick around the place and ride herd on him. He can throw something together for Pop and him at noon."

"Why Hurd?"

"Because he's the only one I can depend on. Tell him I said I'd hold him responsible for Pop."

"I'll tell him," said Trotter, and turned away.

Raiford caught up his horse, threw on Squat's saddle and started for the east hills.

This time he did not follow the path which led to the Circle Cross, but selected a route which would keep him covered by timber and permit him to escape observation from the watcher on the peak. It was Miguel's men who did the watching, but he had no assurance that Squat would not be warned of any approach. Miguel had expressed his dislike of Squat, but Raiford remembered that the Mexican had worked with Armstrong on a mission of murder and refused to take everything he said at face value.

He wanted to surprise Squat and make him a prisoner. In his heart he did not believe that Squat would do any confessing, but when Joe revealed that he had been a Montana marshal and that Squat was a condemned killer in that state, his accusation of Armstrong as Abe Ardell's killer would carry enough weight to cast doubt on the guilt of the Box L. In the meantime he could only hope that in some manner he would find a way to unmask Newt Cragg.

He could, of course, produce the real James Lanier at any time he wished. The young man must be well on his way toward recovery by now, and he could identify both Squat and Miguel as the two who had waylaid and tried to kill him. Then perhaps Miguel could be persuaded to talk. If he refused, at least Newt would have the finger of suspicion pointed at him and would be forced to give up his designs on the Box L. The Double A? Raiford shook his head worriedly. Alice Ardell was loyal to the core; she would most certainly refuse to believe anything against Newt Cragg unless it were backed by unshakable proof.

When Raiford reached the place he had first encountered Squat, he turned into the narrow fissure and reconnoitered the park from its end; but there was no sign of life in the basin and he concluded that Squat had changed his hangout.

Riding down the incline, he offered the killer a free shot, and when that shot was not forthcoming he was certain of the basin's emptiness. His gaze went to the rock where he had left his rifle and then to the shallow gully in which Squat had taken refuge, and he grinned wryly in memory of that evening when each had so carefully and confidently stalked the other. Squat had been so certain of his man that he had actually fired a shot into the shadows below Raiford's balanced rifle.

When he circled the basin he found a narrow exit and went through it to a jumble of rock that eventually led to another park. This too was empty; but when, an hour later, he found still another entrance and another grassy pasture, his cautious approach brought to sight a small herd of cattle. He lay hidden in its entrance until he was certain no human being besides himself was there, then rode down to examine the cattle. There were thirty young steers in the basin and they all wore the Box L brand.

Well, that definitely cleared up one point. The stolen Box L stuff was being hidden here in the hills and common sense said that Miguel Rosas was the thief. Newt's original purpose, Raiford was sure, was to encourage the rustling in order to make trouble between the two outfits, trouble which he hoped would lead to open conflict and the death of Abe Ardell. The cattle were to go to Rosas for his very necessary help. When the Box L became Newt's, a swift raid on the Circle Cross would reveal the stolen animals and in the fight which was sure to follow, Miguel would be eliminated. The cattle, of course, would go back to the Box L. There was no getting around it;

Newt Cragg was clever and had provided for every contingency.

It was noon when Raiford reached the entrance to Miguel's headquarters, and he circled the place in order to approach it from the far side. He noticed a number of Mexicans moving about, but no sight of Squat was to be had and at last he descended into the basin.

He was seen at once, and Miguel himself came from a hut to meet him.

"You are jus' in tam for the *comida*," said Rosas. "You mus' be my guest. Juan! The *señor's caballo*; see that he is fed and cared for. Then take my message to Ricardo. Come weeth me, Señor—Lanier, no?"

"That's right. Much obliged."

He surrendered his horse to the *vaquero* and went into the cabin with Miguel. He entered it warily in case he should find Squat there, but except for a comely Mexican girl the place had no occupants. Miguel waved him to a seat at the table and the girl served them.

"I'm t'ink," said Miguel, "dat you are come for the *Señor* Strongarm. The las' tam you find heem he is make the monkey of you, no?"

"I'd say we made monkeys of each other," said Raiford and told him what had happened.

Miguel nodded, observing Raiford with keen, shrewd eyes. Joe had already appraised him as a clever rascal who would fall in with the plans of another only to the extent that it spelled profit for himself.

"Ees bad *hombre*, thees Squat," the Mexican said. "I'm mos' 'appy eef you e-shoot heem full weeth the 'ole."

"I'll do just that if you tell me where to find him."

"That I cannot do."

"You know where he is," said Raiford boldly. "How does Newt get in touch with him?"

The Mexican observed him under half-closed lids. "Ha! You know dat, eh? Sure I'm fin' heem for Newt. There ees the place where I put the note; every day Squat go there and look. But I'm not tell yet. Someday, yes. Den you wait dere and e-shoot the *Señor* Strongarm full of the 'ole."

"Why not today and get it over with?"

"No. Miguel too ees sit in the game. Today is not the tam."

Raiford recognized finality in his tone. "Have you seen him since the last time I was here?"

"One tam only. He come here for the food. He takes the beeg bag and feel heem full and ride away. He's got the rag aroun' one 'and and there ees blood on the rag. When I ask, he says she ees scratch on the rock."

"He scratched it on a bullet. My bullet."

"Ees ver' bad that the *caballo* ees not use to the gon."

66

"I'm riding one now that won't shy. I'd like to meet up with Squat, but if you won't tell me how to find him I'll just have to keep poking around until I run into him." He tried a flank attack. "By the way, I haven't seen Newt lately; how is his plan coming along?"

The sharp eyes narrowed. "You don' know?"

"Not everything. I'm sort of playing in the dark. Between you and me, Miguel, just what is he up to?"

"Newt, she's the nice man, no?"

Raiford played another hunch. "No, he isn't. He's a damned sneak. Of the two, I prefer Squat. He does his killing in the open."

Miguel munched his *frijoles* thoughtfully, then fixed his level gaze on Raiford and spoke. "The *señor* and Miguel 'ave some t'ings een common. We don' lak the *Señor* Strongarm and we don' lak the *Señor* Cragg. Ees Newt who sen' Squat to me. 'Miguel,' he ees say, 'thees man ees the frien' of me and he 'as no 'ome. You do me the favor and tak heem to your *rancho*.' Thees I do, and what 'appen? He's take what he want and act lak the beeg boss; he beat my *vaqueros* and 'elp heemself to my woman. And eef somebody do not lak what he do, he e-shoot dem." He swallowed some more *frijoles*, then added casually, "Eef you not keel heem, I t'ink I do eet myself."

"Just lead me to him and there won't be any 'if' about it."

Miguel nodded his approval and went on, talking between mouthfuls, making gestures with his knife.

"The *Señor* Cragg. I'm work for heem. Planty tam. How he treat me? Lak the *peon!* Me—Miguel Rosas! I'm *caballero;* I'm got the *rancho*, the cow, the 'orse. I'm good as she, but what he tell me? Nossing! 'Miguel, you do thees, you do dat. I pay so moch.' Dat ees all. He's tell thees beeg *cochino*, Strongarm, but he don' tell Miguel Rosas." He scooped up a knifeful of beans and rammed them into his mouth. "But I'm feex heem; I'm feex heem good! He's not so smart as he t'ink. Me, I got the ace een the 'ole, and when Newt she's mak the bet, I'm raise heem the limit and den I show heem the ace in the 'ole. And den I laff—right een my face!"

Raiford felt his blood begin to pound. If he could crack this Mexican he felt that he could pin Newt Cragg to the mat.

"I don't blame you, *amigo*. I'd like to help. Newt won't tell me anything either. I've guessed a lot, but I need more. Show me that ace in the hole. Newt's out to get his at our expense. We do the dirty work and he gathers the profit. And then when he's through with us, out we go. Just like—James Lanier." He was bending over the table, holding Miguel by the intensity of his gaze.

Sharp suspicion flamed in Rosas' eyes. "He tell you dat, eh?"

"He's told me nothing. But I can use my head for something

else than a hatrack. Newt wants the Double A and thinks he'll get it through Alice Ardell. Squat rubbed out Abe and now that's all set. He wants the Box L, too, and plans to get it through the fake son he palmed off on Pop Lanier. I can guess that because I know, and I think you know, too, that I'm not James Lanier. He wouldn't take the chance of the real son showing up, so he must have had him put out of the way. You're getting a bunch of nice Box L cattle. Why? For putting the real son away for him?"

Miguel stared for a moment; then, to Raiford's surprise, he chuckled.

"No, I'm not put the real Jeem Lanier away. But you are guess pretty good. I'm know thees Jeem Lanier when he's the boy; mebbe I point heem out to somebody, no? You are not heem, so I'm guess too." He abruptly changed the subject. "You 'ave the fire on the Box L, no?"

"Who told you?"

"I'm see eet een the night. The ol' man, he's wake op too late, huh?"

"Try *your* hand at guessing, Miguel."

"*Muy bien!* Pop Lanier, she's the light sleeper. She wake op all right, but she's find heemself tired to de bed. How am I guess?"

"Pretty good. But Newt played it safer. Pop is a light sleeper and he sleeps with his gun. Getting near enough to him to tie him up might have called for a slug in an inconvenient place. Newt started the fire, then nailed the door shut, and while Pop was trying to figure the hammering out, ran around, climbed on a box and spiked a plank across the window."

Miguel smiled in appreciation. "He's smart mans. Ver' smart. You wan' play the joke on heem? When the *Señor* Pop ees die and Newt says he wants to buy the *rancho,* you say no. Me, I t'row my ace een the 'ole in the discard and we are partners. Make lot of money."

"Yeah? And how long do you think we'd live to enjoy it?" Miguel shrugged. "Ees the chance we tak."

"Not me. The odds are too long against us."

"Den what you do?"

"Get the goods on him. I can do it with your help. Show me the ace in the hole, Miguel."

"Ees not tam, my frien'. Lak weeth the *Señor* Strongarm, I mus' wait. The pot, she ees not yet beeg enough. Pretty soon, though, I show you."

That, Raiford knew, was definite and final. He finished his meal and departed, riding through the gap by which he had entered and continuing to the second park with the log cabin where he had heard the peculiar thump. The place was not empty now; through the open doorway he could see two Mexicans partaking of their noon-day meal, and one of them was the *vaquero* who had taken his horse. Had he ridden here to warn the other of Raiford's presence in the basin? Had Miguel invited him to dinner in order to stall for time?

He rode to the doorway and exchanged greetings with the men, scanning the interior as he did so. The men were alone in the room and after riding completely around the cabin Raiford continued his course. He rode until the lowering sun told him that he must turn back if he wished to reach the Box L before dark. Discouragement settled upon him; the hills were so vast, so filled with hiding places, so broken and uneven. Squat might be searching for him diligently as he was searching for Squat and still the two men might never meet. Miguel could put him in touch with Squat if he wished, but the wily Mexican was playing a game of his own and was not ready for the final showdown.

What was Miguel's ace in the hole? Some bit of knowledge, some concrete evidence of Newt's guilt, in all probability. Or would he, at the proper moment, tell of Newt's plan to remove the real James Lanier? Hardly that! it would implicate Miguel himself unless he were adroit enough to pin the whole blame for the shooting on Squat.

Raiford finally turned back, dismissing Squat from his mind in an effort to foresee Newt's next move. The arrival of the fake James Lanier sent down by Jake Rails would complicate matters and, perhaps, bring the whole thing to a head. Where was the fellow? He should have put in an appearance long before this. But he hadn't, or else Newt would have taken steps to put him, Raiford, out of the way.

What would Newt do next? Nearly a week had passed since his attempt to burn Pop Lanier to death. He had set the fire when he had known nobody was on the spread but Pop. The men were away again today, working at the far end of the range; and Joe had told Trotter that he, too, would be gone. But even if Trotter got in touch with Newt to tell him this, he must also tell him that Hurd was with Pop and had been instructed not to leave him for a minute. That should put a crimp in Newt's plans, for whatever he did he must do it unseen.

A vague uneasiness gripped Raiford. Suppose Hurd did stand in his way; Hurd didn't know of Newt's plan. If the man rode out to the Box L, Hurd would have no reason to suspect him. And if only Hurd stood between Newt and the success of his second attempt on Pop's life, Newt would not hesitate to shoot the man in the back in order to remove him as a witness.

Raiford's uneasiness became near panic. He spurred his horse to a run, ignoring the danger of the bad footing beneath him.

10

TROTTER'S RESENTMENT had reached the boiling point. It was bad enough to have to go to the southwest pasture and string fence; it was gall and wormwood to know that while he was doing it Hurd could sit on his tail and read the paper, his only task being to cock an occasional eye at Pop Lanier and feed the old fellow at noontime.

The more Trotter thought of it the hotter burned his resentment, and by the time he reached the mess shack his mind was made up. He went inside and stood by a window watching until Raiford rode out of the yard, then he spoke to Hurd who was just mopping up his breakfast plate.

"I'm supposed to stick around and keep an eye on Pop. You're to take the crew to the southwest pasture and finish up the fence. Take cookie and the chuck wagon with you and don't come in for dinner."

"You makin' me straw boss?" asked Hurd in surprise.

"The boss is! not me. Get 'em movin' out of here."

Hurd took charge, and within half an hour a wagon was loaded with posts and wire, the team was hitched to the stocked chuck wagon, and the whole lot of them were riding from the yard.

Trotter brought the most comfortable chair from the bunkhouse, found an old newspaper with plenty of advertisements in it, and settled himself for a day of ease and luxury. Pop had come out onto the porch of the cabin and was sitting in his chair, hands on its arms, staring straight ahead of him as was his habit. After a while Trotter grew drowsy, so he got up, yawned and stretched and went into the bunkhouse to lounge on his bunk.

After a couple of hours of this the minutes began to drag and Trotter grew restless. He filled in the time until noon by cleaning his guns, doing a little patchwork on his equipment, and strolling aimlessly about the ranch buildings. At noon he went into the cook shack, warmed up some leftovers, made coffee, and took some of the grub over to Pop, eating the rest himself.

When he had finished he went back to the bunkhouse and sat down again. He saw Pop feel his way to the porch, wiping his mouth on the back of his hand, and lower himself into the chair for his after-dinner nap.

Trotter growled an impatient oath. The hell with this! What was the use of hanging around playing nurse to this old maverick? Lanier was good for a couple of hours. If he wanted to ride that ancient bay of his he wouldn't be awake until three o'clock or after. Now was a good time to go to town and get outside a few drinks. Trotter went down to the corral, caught up and saddled his horse, and rode him at a quiet walk from the yard. When he had put a mile between him and the blind man he kicked the horse into a run.

He pulled up before the Royal Flush, tied and went inside. There were a half dozen loafers at the bar and he joined them. He bought a round of drinks, somebody reciprocated, and then somebody else. Trotter began to feel good. Why go back at all until just before the crew were due to arrive? Pop would probably holler for him to saddle the bay, but he could say that he was working somewhere and did not hear him. The hell with the old coot.

Across the street, Newt Cragg looked through his office window and saw the Box L horse at the hitching rail. He knew it belonged to Trotter and wondered what had brought him to town. He crossed the street and entered the Royal Flush.

He slid in beside Trotter and asked, "Boss give you a day off?"

"Naw. He left me to ride herd on Pop while the crew string fence on the southwest pasture. I got tired sittin' on my tail and come in for a few quick ones."

Newt's eyes widened slightly, then narrowed again. He said, "Don't blame you; you'll never be missed. Might as well get all you can out of it. Where's young Lanier?"

"Went somewhere for the day. Said he had business. Told me to leave Hurd at the house to watch Pop, but what t'hell. Hurd's always gettin' the soft jobs. I figured I could watch out for Pop just as good and sent Hurd out with the boys. They took the chuck wagon and won't be in till dark."

"Jim mention the nature of his business?"

"Naw. But he headed for the east hills. I figger he's goin' snoopin' around the Circle Cross. You reckon he's wise to Rosas?"

Newt thought it quite likely, but did not tell Trotter so.

"Why should he be wise? And if he is, what of it? They'll spot him long before he gets close and steer him away from any dangerous locality. Don't worry about it."

He drew out a thick silver watch and scanned it.

"I've got to ride some twenty miles north to get some papers I left for a client to sign. Couldn't find him the other day and left them; now I've got to pick them up. You might as well stay here and enjoy yourself." He called the bartender, "Sam! Another round for the boys and one for myself. I've got forty miles to ride and need fortification."

He wanted them to hear the announcement; it would bolster his alibi.

He downed his drink and hurried out. His face was set in lines of purposefulness as he crossed the street. This was the chance he had been waiting for; what was to be done must be done now. The fake son was somewhere in the east hills, the crew were in a remote southwest pasture. Trotter was in town. Pop Lanier was alone at the ranch.

He saddled up swiftly, mounted and rode around into the street. He crossed to the Royal Flush, dismounted and once more went inside. Trotter was still there and gave every indication of remaining there the rest of the afternoon. Newt called for another round, went outside and got into his saddle and rode slowly past the saloon, headed north. He wanted them to see him leave.

He held to the northward course until he was well out of town, then he began his circle, cutting wide of Calixto, keeping ridge or timber between himself and the town. He skirted the base of the eastern hills, making the best speed he could. He sighted nobody anywhere and grew bolder. He essayed a short cut over open range and was nearly across it when he saw a horse. It was some distance away, standing by the road which led from the valley ranches to Calixto; but although he could discern a saddle on the horse he could not see the rider. Then, through some brush which screened the animal's legs, he caught the movement of a colored scarf. The rider was stooping or kneeling, and, Newt decided, was busy removing a stone from the frog of a hoof. So absorbed was he in his task that Newt was sure he had not seen him.

There was a gully close by, and Newt backed his horse a step at a time until he reached its brim; then he wheeled the animal and sent him down the bank, and from then on was careful to keep out of sight of the road. He walked his horse into the Box L yard, his eyes darting about him, searching, prying. There was nobody about the place but Pop Lanier, and he was asleep in his chair, his chin on his chest. As Newt approached the cabin Pop's head jerked up and his blind eyes opened.

"That you, Trotter? Saddle up my horse; I'm goin' for a ride. Damn this settin' around and sleeping my life away. You hear me? Saddle up."

Newt dismounted and dropped his rein.

"No, Pop, it's not Trotter. It's Newt. Trotter's around somewhere, but I can saddle up for you. Fact is, I wanted to ask a few questions about that fire. I'll ride along with you. We can talk as we ride."

"Newt, huh?" The old man's face was hard and suspicious. "I reckon mebbe I might want to talk to you, too. Saddle up and let's get goin'."

He got up and shuffled into the cabin and Newt led his horse down to the corral. Here he swiftly off-saddled and turned the animal into the inclosure, then caught another one and put his rig upon it. The use of a Box L horse was part of his plan; the prints which paralleled those of the bay must not be those of his own horse. He tied it, got Pop's rig, then caught up and saddled the bay. He led both horses to the cabin.

Pop stood on the porch waiting for him, and Newt saw that the old man was wearing his six-gun. Newt's eyes narrowed. So the old boy was suspicious of him. Why? Had he begun to suspect the truth? Had he discovered that his supposed son was a fake? Or had that meddling fellow told him things?

He pretended not to notice the armament. He steered the bay to the edge of the porch and put the rein in Pop's hand. Pop stepped into the saddle and they started off at a walk. When they were half a mile from the house and were headed for the east hills Newt said, "Now tell me about the fire. I'm curious. What started it? Smoke your pipe in bed and go to sleep?"

"I ain't that much of a fool," snapped Pop. "Take me for a danged tenderfoot? No; the fire was set."

Newt pretended shocked surprise. "Who would do a thing like that?"

"Who do you think? They'd just planted Abe, hadn't they? Who do you think done it?"

"Not the Double A! I can't believe that."

"Neither does Jim; but, by grab! they ain't foolin' me. And what's more, whoever it was that set it, the lousy son nailed me in so's I couldn't get out."

This time Newt reined his horse to a sudden halt as though completely overcome; but there was a cynical grin on his face instead of the surprise which would have been there had Pop been able to see.

He said, "No!" and made it sound incredulous.

"Come on, come on; what you stoppin' for? Sure they nailed me in. They had to. I can get around. They knew I'd get out if they didn't nail me in."

Newt spurred up beside him. "Tell me all about it."

So Pop elaborated, and as he did so Newt began crowding the bay, turning the animal gradually in the direction he wished him to go. He wasn't listening to Pop's vehement words; his eyes were fixed on a distant gray patch against the side of the mountain, the scar of rock left when a huge section of earth had split off and fallen centuries before, leaving an abrupt drop of several hundred feet with a mass of jagged rocks at its base. A path angled up the hill and along a ledge at the top of the cliff. The path was narrow, there being just room for two horsemen to pass. Newt kept crowding the bay until they were headed for the foot of the path, glancing quickly about him occasionally to be sure that there was no person abroad to observe. If someone were to come in sight the deal was off; Newt would immediately turn back and take the old man safely into the Box L yard. He was a patient man as well as a cautious one; there must be no witnesses to what must happen, no matter how long or how often the thing must be postponed.

But nobody appeared to spoil his plan, and Pop finished his story and Newt expressed his incredulity and then allowed himself to be convinced that Pop was probably right.

When the subject had been exhausted, Pop changed the conversation.

"Jim says it ain't the Double A that's stealin' our stuff."

Newt glanced at him sharply, but the impassive face told him nothing.

"He does? Who else could it be? What about that Double A calf getting its dinner from a Box L cow?"

"Says it coulda been planted to throw the blame on the Double A. Claims it's Rosas that's doin' the rustlin'."

So that explained the fellow's journey into the eastern hills! Always troublesome, this fake James Lanier was becoming quite a nuisance. Well, today the thing must be concluded. Then for the showdown and—pay-off.

They were nearing the path now and Newt's eyes narrowed in contemplation.

"It could be Rosas at that," he admitted with apparent reluctance. "I never thought of him. That Double A calf held my attention, as it was probably intended to." He seemed to think for a moment. "I wish you weren't blind," he said abruptly.

"You sure of that?" sneered the old man.

Newt ignored the implication. "Of course. If you could see to ride that far we'd go right up to the Circle Cross and look it over. But it's too much for a helpless old man."

Pop picked that up, as Newt had known he would. "Who's helpless? I can't see, but I can hear and I can ride and shoot. Give me a sound to shoot at and I'll hit whatever made the sound. We're goin' up there right now. If you're man enough to rassle down a steer with a Box L on it, I can feel the brand with my fingers."

"I'm afraid it would be too much for you," said Newt gently.

"Too much yore grandmaw! I can ride as far as a tenderfoot like you and shoot a heap straighter even if I can't see. Where are we?"

"'At the foot of the path that leads up to the Circle Cross. We'd have to cross that narrow ledge, and—"

"Think I don't know? Start up that path. My hoss can see better'n you. Where's the path? Steer me into it."

Newt smiled tightly. "All right, if you insist. I'm all for it myself. Left a bit and you can't miss it."

The bay found the path and Newt fell in behind. They

started the climb. Pop was growling, "Thinks I'm a sissy! I'll show him, by jacks!"

He gave the horse its head and the wise animal went up the path. Newt followed, his narrowed eyes scanning the range above which they were lifting themselves. It was barren of human beings. They reached the narrow ledge and started across it.

Newt began to sweat. The time was approaching and, callous as he was, determined as he was, he dreaded what he had to do. But he knew he must not falter now. His face was dead white and his eyes glittered feverishly. His muscles twitched. They were nearing the middle of the ledge. A few more steps—!

"How far are we across?" asked Pop over his shoulder. Newt forced the words out. "Not quite—half—way."

"Scared, ain't you?" sneered Pop. "Who's the sissy now?"

"Yes, I'm scared. It's a long drop."

Pop cackled. "Ain't the fall that hurts, it's the sudden stop."

The mountain rose on their right; on their left was the three-hundred-foot drop. And at the end of that drop were sharp, jagged rocks. No matter how lucky a man was he could never hope to survive that fall.

Newt edged his horse forward, nudging between the wall on his right and Pop's horse. The head of Newt's mount reached a point opposite Pop's leg.

Pop half turned. "Hey! Quit crowdin'. Fall back and leave it to yore hoss, you danged fool!"

Newt touched the horse with his spurs and jumped him two feet farther. Pop's bay staggered but recovered his footing quickly. Pop's hand dropped to the gun at his hip, but Newt reached the weapon first. He yanked it from its holster. "No, you don't!" he said, and his voice was a croak.

Pop reined the bay to a halt. "What you doin'? Gimme my gun and get back where you belong!"

"Not this time!" Newt's voice was shrill now. "You've given your last order, you old buzzard!"

"Get back, I say!" Pop was screaming too. He flung his right arm in a backward swipe that caught Newt on the mouth and nearly knocked him from his saddle. "Jim warned me about you! He said you was playin' me for a sucker!"

They were his last words. Newt no longer had to drive himself; his reaction to the blow was instinctive. Pop drove his spurs deep in an effort to pull away, but Newt was just a second ahead of him. His horse leaped an instant before Lanier's and a thousand pounds of bone and muscle struck the shoulder of the bay. The animal trumpeted wildly, crying its fear, then it went over the edge, forefeet pawing frantically.

Newt's horse lunged ahead and the lawyer shut his eyes

and clenched his teeth and sagged over in his saddle.

The horn jolted him at every leap, but he suffered it, and not until they were across the ledge and hoofs pounded on soft turf did he open his eyes and sit upright. They were among the trees again, with the hill sloping gently away on his left. Newt pulled the horse to a walk and angled downward towards the base of the mountain. He felt shaken and sick, but slowly the feeling faded and was replaced by a growing sense of exultation. It was done! He had not dreamed that it would be so hard, so terrifying, but he had done it. By the time he reached the range he was feeling quite proud of himself.

He did not go near the foot of the cliff. When he was in a position to observe it he halted and looked. He saw the horse and, a short distance away, the man. Both were sprawled awkwardly; both were utterly motionless. But he had to be sure. He drew a pair of glasses from his saddle pocket and focused them. His hands trembled and he began to sweat again, but he summoned all his will power and finally steadied himself.

There was no doubt of it; both man and horse were dead.

He sighed a great sigh of relief, replaced the glasses, then unfolded a handkerchief and mopped his dripping face. He rode directly to the ranch, his eyes continuing to probe. He approached cautiously, looking over the terrain from every angle. It was quiet and deserted. He dropped weakly from the horse, stripped it and turned it into the corral. He got his own horse and saddled it, then mounted and headed in the direction of Calixto. He circled the town and struck northward. He must not return until late that night; a man didn't ride forty miles in a few hours.

He was perfectly safe; he knew it. But it is the little things that count, and he must be thorough. His alibi must hold.

11

IN HIS ENDEAVOR to reach the ranch in the shortest possible time, Raiford almost immediately ran into difficulties. Deciding that the way back could be considerably shortened, he started southwestward, using the peak for his guide and aiming for a point which he judged to be directly north of the Box L. He presently found himself in such upended terrain that he knew his decision had been a poor one; nevertheless he pressed onward, that uneasy premonition of danger to Pop Lanier growing upon him.

There were steep hills to be detoured and rocky flats to be crossed in a winding course which almost doubled the distance, but finally he came to a deep gash in the earth which extended as far as he could see and which offered as an alternative to many miles' riding a descent which was almost perpendicular and an ascent on the far side even more difficult of negotiation. Pressed by the need for haste, he chose the more direct method, angling down the face of the canyon wall, his horse slipping and sliding. The last hundred yards were accomplished by riding an avalanche which separated man and beast and sent both rolling into the rubble below.

When Raiford finally got the horse on its feet, he found that it had pulled a tendon and limped badly. There was nothing to do but lead it along the rocky bed until he reached a point where the cliff receded and the animal could make the ascent. After that the way smoothed out and he was able to ride, although he had to hold the horse to a painful walk.

When at last he entered the Box L yard, the crew had come in, had eaten, and were in the bunkhouse. Pop was not on the cabin porch, and Raiford scanned the corral as he stripped his horse. The bay was not there; Pop had gone for his daily ride. Dusk was turning to darkness and Raiford felt worried; but he remembered that darkness meant nothing to Pop, and that the bay could find its way as easily as he could by daylight.

He rubbed his horse's injured leg with liniment, turned him into the corral and fed him, then went to the cabin to prepare his supper. Pop had not returned by the time he had finished, and he went down to the bunkhouse to inquire about him. Trotter and four of the men were playing poker at the table beneath the hanging lamp; Hurd was stretched out on his bunk reading a paper by the same light.

Raiford went to Hurd's bunk and said, "How long has Pop been riding?"

Hurd looked up. "I don't know. He was gone when we came in."

"When you came in? I left orders for you to stick around the house and keep an eye on Pop."

"First I heard of it. After you left Trotter told me to take the crew to the southwest pasture and string fence. Said you'd ordered him to stay here with Pop."

A sudden wave of anger swept over Raiford, the hotter because he knew now that his premonition regarding Pop had been justified. He swung about to glare at Trotter over the table. Trotter had put down his cards and was staring back at him, his heavy face twisted in a belligerent scowl.

Raiford said harshly, "You damned gorilla! Why didn't you carry out my orders?"

"Because I'm done takin' orders from you! I'm foreman of this outfit; I'll give the orders to my men. I told Hurd to take the crew out and I stayed here myself."

"We'll see about that later. Right now I want to know what time Pop went for his ride."

"I don't know. I don't give a damn. He was gone when I got back."

"Got back from where?"

"From town."

Raiford's rage against this insolent bully was growing, but he held it in check. "When did you go and what time did you get back?"

Trotter became more confident, more cocky. "I don't carry no watch. I fixed the old coot his dinner and left when he was takin' a nap. I come home just before sundown."

"My orders were that Pop wasn't to be left alone a minute, night or day."

"So what? I ain't being paid to ride herd on no sourpuss like him."

"Why you're being paid at all is a mystery to me. You're done as foreman. If you can't take orders, you can't give them. Hurd'll take over from here on."

"Hurd! Why, you lousy—!"

Trotter pushed the table back and came to his feet, his chair going over behind him. He rounded the table in three strides and hurled himself at Raiford. The charge was like that of an elephant, ponderous but irresistible, and under the sheer weight of the impact Raiford was hurled back half a dozen paces. A heavy fist planted squarely on his jaw speeded his backward progress; it dazed him and he nearly went down. He regained his balance and tried to shake off the fog which clung to his head. Trotter hit him again, a glancing blow this time, and once more he became Montana Joe, gold-town marshal.

He stepped to one side and Trotter passed him, carried by his own momentum. Two of the men grabbed the table and pulled it out of the way. They were in the aisle between the bunks, a space six feet wide and as long as the building. Trotter turned and made another rush, and again Raiford avoided him. The men crowded back on the bunks or against them, their faces showing their appreciation of a good rough-and-tumble fight. There was no sympathy for either of the contestants; they gave no more loyalty to Trotter or Raiford than they gave to any man.

Trotter turned and halted, sensing that the lighter, quicker man was making a fool of him.

"Come and get it, you yellabelly!" he challenged.

Raiford stood there watching him, measuring him. That one blow had been a paralyzing one and he needed time to rid himself of its effects. One more like it would spell a quick end. He must make the man come to him.

Trotter did just that. Infuriated by the failure of his taunt, confident of the power in his mighty arms, Trotter lunged forward in another attack. But Raiford was ready for him now.

He ducked under the flailing arms and came up braced, chest to chest with Trotter. The big man stopped at the impact as though he had crashed into a stone wall. The recoil sent him back a foot, and Raiford's fist came up in a vicious blow that caught him under the chin and blasted him to the soles of his boots.

And now Raiford waded in, stabbing at the tortured jaw, ignoring the wild blows that the weakened Trotter tried to throw, crowding him so closely that the huge fists at the ends of the pumping arms found only the emptiness behind his head. He beat a tattoo on Trotter's midsection, his fist sinking into the softness of Trotter's belly, and the man kept backing away down the aisle, his breath coming in tortured grunts, the confidence in his mean little eyes melting into apprehension and uncertainty.

He tangled with his own overturned chair and went down on his back, and Raiford, not daring to give him time to recover, went down with him, still punching. There were no rules in this bout; they fought it out on the floor, rolling and kicking and gouging. Raiford shifted his attack to the man's face, driving short powerful blows to the massive chin and heavy cheeks.

It was too much punishment for even the mammoth Trotter. His retaliating blows became feebler, wilder; his eyes turned glassy. He was flat on his back, his chest heaving in short, panting breaths. Raiford rolled clear of him, lay on his side and brought his right up in a powerful uppercut that caught Trotter flush on the button. Trotter gave a final grunt and went lax.

Raiford got to his feet, turned and let his eyes seek out each of them in turn. "Anybody feel like taking it up where he left off?"

Nobody answered but Hurd. He had got off his bunk and was standing beside it, grinning. "Not me, thanks," he said; then, *"Look out!"*

He leaped even as Raiford spun about.

It was incredible, but Trotter had already regained consciousness. He was still on the floor, braced by his left elbow. His right hand was drawing the six-gun from its holster and the lust to kill shone in his eyes.

Hurd threw himself at Trotter in a long dive, gripping the man's gun wrist with both hands, throwing the weapon out of line. Trotter snarled an oath, gave the arm a mighty wrench and tore loose. But he had lost his chance. Raiford leaped forward and kicked, the gun went spinning end over end through the doorway and into the darkness outside. His own Colt came out and leveled at the prostrate man.

"Thanks, Hurd," he said. "I guess you can get up now."

Trotter still glared defiantly up at Raiford. "Go ahead and shoot. Shoot and be damned!"

"You're safe enough as long as you answer my questions. Did you saddle up for Pop before you left for town?"

"Naw. I told you he was asleep."

"Anybody see you when you were in town?"

"Nobody but the bartender at the Royal Flush and about eight others, includin' Newt Cragg."

"You were there all afternoon?"

"Yeah."

"How about Newt?"

"He left right after I got there. Said he hadda ride north twenty miles to pick up some papers."

"Did he?"

"If you mean did he pick up the papers, how in hell would I know? He rode out of Calixto, headin' north. He wasn't back when I left." Some of Trotter's defiance returned. "How about yourself? You're mighty good at askin' questions, how are you at answerin' 'em? Where were you this afternoon?"

"You're the one that's on the spot, not me. You disobeyed orders in the first place, and now you're responsible if Pop rode off somewhere and got hurt."

He lowered his gun and turned to the others. "Somebody saddled up for Pop. He couldn't catch up that bay and do it himself. Who was it?"

They looked at each other wonderingly, and Hurd said, "If Trotter didn't do it, I can't figure who did. The rest of us were on the job in that southwest pasture, includin' the cook. I'll take my oath on that."

"Well, let's get saddled up. We've got to look for him even if it is dark. That bay might have ditched him."

"He broke a leg doin' it then," observed Hurd grimly, "or we'd sure enough find him outside the feed shed."

Raiford was in agreement with him. There was little doubt in his mind that Pop had met with an accident, in all probability a fatal one. Nevertheless, they must go through the motions.

They saddled up in the dark and rode across the range in the direction generally taken by Pop. They spread out in a thin line, walking their horses and keeping contact by calling to each other occasionally. When they had covered several miles in this manner Raiford called the search off for the night. There was too much ground to cover and there was no moonlight to help them.

He turned in with the shadow of grim foreboding hanging over him. Beneath this feeling was one of fury and frustration. If Pop had met with foul play Newt Cragg was responsible, yet Joe had not a single item of tangible evidence that would implicate the man. He had the real James Lanier, but Newt could successfully deny any part in the attempted murder of that young man unless Squat or Miguel were to testify against him. Raiford was certain Squat would not talk, and it was unlikely that Miguel would unless he saw some profit in it for himself. Miguel was playing his own game. The stolen cattle were going to the Circle Cross, but again Newt could plead ignorance of that fact. Trotter had been hired to make trouble between the two outfits, but the likelihood of his openly admitting it was about as remote as a snowstorm in Ecuador.

Raiford slept that night with the haunting, sightless eyes of Pop Lanier staring accusingly at him.

They renewed their search immediately after breakfast the next morning, and now that it was daylight they had no trouble in shaping their course. They started at the porch of the cabin, where they found tracks which Hurd declared were made by the bay. They followed these out of the yard and noticed at once that another pair paralleled them.

Hurd said, "Well, that makes it look better for Pop. Somebody rode with him, so likely he's all right. I figure he went away on a visit, and the feller who went with him will fetch him back some time today."

Raiford had his doubts, but did not express them.

They followed the tracks in an easterly direction, and presently Raiford found himself gazing at a gray scar on the side of the mountain where rock falls and erosion had worn a perpendicular cliff.

"Funny they'd ride in this direction," Hurd said. "There's no road out here that leads anywhere except a trail across the hills. . . . What's the matter?"

For Raiford had reined in, his eyes fixed on the base of the gray scar, his face as hard as the rock at which he gazed. Without answering he uttered an oath and put his horse to a run. They followed, wondering.

Long before they reached the base of the cliff they ceased to wonder. They saw a patch of reddish brown which finally resolved itself into the shape of a dead horse, and when they drew near a pair of sightless eyes stared at them from the white face of Pop Lanier. His head was cocked at such an angle that they knew the neck which supported it had snapped.

Raiford halted them at the base of the rubble and cautioned them to be on the lookout for prints. They dismounted and picked their way to where Pop and the horse lay. There was sufficient dust to hold impressions, but they found none of any kind.

For a short time nobody spoke. They looked at Pop and the horse, and reached the conclusion that they were expected to reach; then, of one accord, they raised their eyes to the edge of the cliff three hundred feet above.

"Now what was he doin' ridin' up there?" one of them wondered aloud. "And what come over that crazy bay? Pop mighta been blind, but the hoss wasn't."

"No," repeated Raiford grimly, "the horse wasn't. What we should be asking is who was it that pushed Pop off that ledge."

Startled, they switched their gazes to him.

"*Pushed* him off!" said Hurd.

"It's pretty plain, isn't it? Pop went riding with somebody. That somebody was still with him a mile back where we left the trail. He'd certainly know better than to turn a blind man loose so far from home, and if he rode up to that ledge with Pop and Pop's horse went over by accident he'd certainly report it. But Pop went over and he didn't say a thing about it."

"Maybe he did leave Pop and Pop got turned around and wandered up there and fell off."

Raiford did not argue the point. He believed he knew just what had happened, but, as in the case of the fire, he had no proof. "We can soon find out," he said, and led the way back to where they had left the tracks.

They followed the two pairs of prints to the foot of the hill and into the trail which angled up its side. When they reached the ledge Raiford halted them, and, dismounting, went ahead on foot. On the rocky ledge he lost the tracks, but somewhere about halfway across he found fresh scratches where the hoofs of Pop's bay had gone over the edge.

Raiford went back, reported what he had found, and the whole party rode over the ledge. On the far side, where the ground was soft, they saw deep tracks which were made by a rapidly running horse. Well beyond the ledge the animal had been abruptly halted; from there the tracks led down the side of the mountain and out onto the open range.

Raiford reconstructed the scene for them. "He pushed Pop over the edge and then got panicky. He raced his horse across the ledge, and when he was safe in the trees he pulled up. When he got his nerve back, he rode down into the valley, probably to make sure that Pop was dead."

They had nothing to say to this and the party silently continued the track of the second horse. The trail did not take them near the foot of the cliff; it led them straight back towards the Box L headquarters.

"How'd he know Pop was dead if he didn't go back?" wondered Hurd.

"When you come to think of it, why should he go back? Even if the fall didn't kill Pop, he would have been all stove up. He was blind, without a horse, and miles from the ranch house. He'd die eventually anyway." His voice was bitter.

"There's just one thing that may lead us to the killer. Did you notice the print of the horse he rode?"

"Sure. Broken shoe on the off hind. Dead giveaway."

Yes, thought Raiford, a dead giveaway. Too much so. Entirely too careless for Newt Cragg. Not once had the man made a slip; that he had failed to notice the broken shoe, or to provide for it, was very unlikely.

The tracks led them straight to the corral. At Raiford's order the men dismounted and went inside the inclosure. There were six horses there, including Raiford's, which still limped. One by one they were caught and their feet examined. None of them was wearing a broken shoe.

"That narrows it down to the horses we're riding ourselves," said Raiford. "I know that horse was in this corral, for I've seen its print."

They left the corral and Joe and Hurd together examined the hoofs of each horse ridden by the crew. Trotter, whom Raiford had ordered to come along with them, sneered as they examined his mount. Its shoes were intact in every particular. So were the shoes of the other horses.

Hurd took Raiford to one side. "How about this feller, Trotter? He could have pulled a shoe and used a broken one, then tacked the good one on afterwards."

"I don't think it was Trotter, but we can check his story at the Royal Flush. Of course, he could have done away with Pop in the morning and then put some dirty dishes in the kitchen to make it look as though Pop had eaten his dinner, but somehow I believe he told us a straight story."

"I wouldn't believe that jigger if he swore to his story on the body of his dead mother," said Hurd shortly. "Pop might have eaten the dinner at that. He was blind and didn't know what time it was. Trotter could have fed him two hours early and told him it was noon."

They walked back to rejoin the men. They were gathered in a little knot beside the horse Raiford had ridden, and as Joe approached Trotter looked at him with triumph in his eyes.

"Ain't no chance that *two* hosses could be wearin' exactly the same kind of busted shoes on their hind hoofs, is there?" he asked.

"Not one in a million," answered Raiford.

Trotter grunted. "That why you didn't examine the feet of yore own horse? I reckon we've found the one who shoved Pop off that cliff." He pointed towards the ground.

Raiford strode forward and pointed at the print, then swiftly raised the horse's hoof and looked at the broken shoe it wore. Then he lowered the foot and stood erect. "This is the horse," he said.

"Yeah. And you're ridin' it."

The men were staring at him. In some of the faces he read indifference, in others curiosity, in a few, accusation.

Hurd said, "Mind explainin', Jim?" His voice was cold.

"No, I don't. This horse was ridden by the one who pushed Pop off the cliff, but I wasn't riding him then. I rode my own horse yesterday. He went lame, as you probably noticed there in the corral. I roped this one and rode him this morning." He looked steadily at the leering Trotter. "Like Trotter here and Newt Cragg, I have an alibi. I was with Miguel Rosas yesterday."

Hurd relaxed. "That suits me. . . . What do we do next?"

"Take the spring wagon out there and fetch Pop in." He turned to Trotter. "As for you, fork your horse and make tracks. You're through. Get your pay from the man who hired you."

"I will," said Trotter. "And after I see him, maybe I'll be back."

He climbed onto his horse and rode briskly from the yard.

12

RAIFORD saw the spring wagon hitched up and on its way after Pop's body, then mounted the horse with the broken shoe and set out for Calixto.

The mystery had built up to its climax, and he knew just what Newt's next move would be and how he must meet it. The feeling of his impotence depressed him; he could nullify Newt's plan so far as the Box L was concerned, but with the ammunition he had he could do nothing more. Newt was guilty of fraud, of conspiracy to commit murder, of murder itself; yet Newt Cragg would go free and even unsuspected unless some way could be found—

Raiford sought for that way as he had sought for it so many times before. He had not found it by the time he reached Calixto.

There were two horses standing at the rail outside Cragg's office. One he knew to be Trotter's; the other wore a Circle Cross brand. A second look told him whose it was; it belonged to Miguel Rosas.

He dismounted before the Royal Flush and went inside. He took the bartender aside and questioned him. Trotter had come in the day before about two o'clock and had remained until around five.

"How about Newt Cragg?"

"Newt? He come in right after Trotter, but he didn't stay. Bought a couple of rounds of drinks and went out, sayin' he had to ride up north somewhere after a paper or somethin'.

He come in a few minutes later and bought another drink, then rode north. Didn't see him again until after nine last night. He said he'd just got back."

"Do you happen to know who he went to see?"

"No, I don't. Why don't you ask him?"

He moved away and that was that. Raiford had no trouble in understanding what had happened. Newt had learned from Trotter that Pop was alone on the ranch and had taken the opportunity he had been waiting for. He had stated his purpose of riding twenty miles north and back again in the presence of the men in the Royal Flush, had set out in a northerly direction and held to that course until he was out of sight of Calixto.

He had circled the town and ridden to the Box L and had found Pop Lanier alone. The ride which followed might have been Newt's suggestion or Pop's; it made no difference. Once in the saddle it would be an easy matter to steer the blind man's horse to that ledge and push it over. The crafty lawyer had even used a Box L horse so that the tracks could not later be connected with his own mount.

Finished with his gruesome business, Newt had returned to within sight of Calixto, then had circled and kept going north until he had ridden a full twenty miles in all, after which he had turned back, confident that the time element had been properly taken care of. Whom he had visited would remain a mystery until he chose to tell. He might even have somebody planted to testify that Newt had actually visited him on the day specified.

The picture was complete, but that was just what it was—a picture pieced together by Raiford's imagination. There was not a single shred of evidence to pin the crime on the lawyer.

Raiford stood at the bar sipping his beer, and presently Trotter came in and slouched up to the bar. He gave Joe a venomous glare, ordered whiskey and stood scowling at his image in the backbar mirror. Raiford finished his drink and went out. His obvious move was to report Pop's death to Newt just as though the lawyer didn't know a thing about it. He crossed the street to the office, saw that Miguel's horse was still at the rail, and went inside.

Newt was seated at his desk, leaning back in the swivel chair, smiling and talking with Rosas. The Mexican lounged in one of the office chairs, hat pushed back on his head, a leg thrown carelessly and gracefully over one of its arms. He stared at Raiford with no sign of recognition in his eyes.

Newt said, "Ah! Good morning, Mr. Lanier. Trotter just brought me the sad news. My condolences. It appears that you are now the owner of the Box L, lock, stock and barrel."

"You don't seem to be taking Pop's death too hard."

"I don't suppose anybody is, yourself included. But there were some things about Pop that I really liked."

"You speaking of his money and his cattle?"

Newt's eyes flicked and hardened. "I think we'd better have a little private chat," he said coldly. *"Señor* Rosas will excuse us if we step back into my quarters for a few minutes, I'm sure."

Miguel smiled lazily and said, "Of a certainty, *Señor* Cragg."

Raiford followed Newt into a back room without any hesitation. He was perfectly safe for the moment; he had something which Newt wanted. The room was small but neatly furnished as a combination kitchen and bedroom. It was very clean. Newt closed the door and seated Raiford in a chair in a remote corner near the bed. Newt sat down on the bed itself.

He said, "I've always wanted to own a cattle ranch like the Box L, and I have a strong hunch that you'd like to sell it. You've been a wanderer, Jim, from the time you were a boy. I think you'd like to keep on wandering."

"I'm not so sure. A fellow gets tired of roaming around, and the Box L is a nice little spread. Maybe I don't want to sell."

"You'll sell, and at my price. That price, as you should know, is $500."

"Not enough, Newt. Not enough by a long shot. If I sell at all the least I'd consider is $20,000."

Newt's eyes were still cold and his voice colder. "You'll sell, and for $500; or you won't live long to enjoy your heritage. All I have to do is point out that you are an impostor and your goose is cooked."

"That wouldn't help you much, would it? You'd have to dig up another fake Jim Lanier, and folks might not accept him so readily a second time."

"It might prove more embarrassing to you than to me. Pop's death has put you on the spot. You and I both know that his fall wasn't accidental, don't we?"

"You certainly do."

"And so do you. Pop's bay never fell off that ledge; it was pushed off. I can easily guess how it happened."

"You shouldn't have to guess very hard."

"That's right; and once you are exposed, other folks won't have to guess very hard either. Let's see if we can reconstruct it." He leaned back on his hands and half closed his eyes. "An unscrupulous young fellow learns that crabby old Pop Lanier is searching for his son, whom he hasn't seen since he was a boy. There's a nice, rich cattle spread just crying for that son to come home and claim it. The unscrupulous young fellow waylays the son on his way home and disposes of him. Then he takes his place and is accepted by the old man."

He paused and looked at Joe, and Raiford said, "You're doing fine; go on with the fairy story."

"When the time is ripe, the fake son sends the crew away to a remote corner of the ranch and announces that he is going to be absent for the day. He leaves the foreman, Trotter, in charge of Pop, knowing very well that Trotter will duck out the first chance he gets. He keeps within sight of the ranch, probably observing what goes on through field glasses, and sees Trotter start for town. The setup is perfect. He hurries home and takes the old man for a ride. When he comes back, he's alone. He hides in the hills until the crew comes in, then returns from his day's journey. He is shocked to find that Pop had met with an accident and indignantly fires Trotter for not staying on the job. But he overlooks one little detail. The horse he is riding has a broken shoe, and the horse that accompanied Pop on the fatal ride also has a broken shoe. The break is the same and the hoof is the same. Remarkable coincidence."

Raiford said, "This fake son is so clever, he'd never make a mistake like that."

"The cleverest of us makes an occasional mistake," said Newt calmly. "As it happens, if this fellow really had been Pop's son he would have been believed had he explained that his own horse was lame and that he took this one out of the corral *after* Pop's death. But when you consider that he's an impostor, that he had done away with the real son, that he stood to gain a rich ranch that otherwise would not be his, and that he has nobody to prove his story that he was absent on business the whole time, only a fool would believe him. I rather imagine that an indignant populace would take him out and hang him by the neck until he was quite dead."

"You're probably right," said Raiford tightly, "especially since our shining legal light would be on hand to do any prompting that might be necessary. But suppose that I could prove my alibi for that afternoon. Suppose that, instead of hanging around the ranch watching, I was miles away in the east hills. What then?"

"Why then," said Newt, and his voice was actually pleasant now, "you would be absolutely in the clear and could even sue me for slander, as well as anybody else who'd made such slanderous accusations. But how would you go about proving that alibi?"

"By the man I was with yesterday afternoon. By Miguel Rosas."

"Rosas?" Newt's eyebrows went up. "I didn't know you were even acquainted with the gentleman. However, we can easily put your alibi to the test." He got up. "If Miguel says you were with him, I'm afraid you've got me in a spot where I must apologize as humbly as I can."

He led the way to the front office and Raiford followed him without enthusiasm. Newt was too ready for that test, and Miguel was as much a rascal as was the lawyer. Still Miguel hated Cragg, or said he did, and might take great pleasure in upsetting Newt's applecart.

The Mexican was still in the office, sitting in the same position, smiling and smoking.

Newt said, "Miguel, this is James Lanier. He tells me he was with you at the Circle Cross yesterday afternoon. How about 't?"

The Mexican observed Raiford with amused eyes. He smiled a broader smile and shook his head gently.

"I am afraid the *señor* ees mistake. I 'ave not the pleasure of his acquaintance. I'm not see heem before thees day."

Raiford didn't bother to call him a liar. He didn't even get angry. Miguel was playing his own game and supporting Joe's alibi was not part of it.

He turned to Newt and said sullenly, "Well, I guess that settles it. What do I do next?"

"Make the necessary arrangements for the funeral. The little grove behind the house would be a nice place to plant Pop. Our local saddle maker has a reputation as a preacher of sorts. Tomorrow morning would be the right time. Meanwhile I'll prepare the deed and have it ready for your signature immediately after the services. The price—but we discussed that, didn't we? Good day, Mr. Lanier."

He was sneering as he bowed Raiford out. Miguel was still smoking, still lounging, still wearing his languid smile.

Raiford found the saddle maker and engaged his services for the following morning; then he mounted and set out for the ranch.

There was no way out of it; he must sign the deed and accept the $500 in payment. His signature, of course, would be no good once he produced the real James Lanier, and he would have the doubtful satisfaction of cheating Newt Cragg of $500. It was at best a poor kind of satisfaction.

He swore in anger and frustration. He had to find a way to expose this slick shyster. But he was damned if he knew how to do it.

13

HE WAS STILL GROPING frantically for ideas when he reached the Box L. He put up his horse and went into the little cabin. They had brought Pop in and had prepared him for burial.

He lay on his bunk, hands crossed on his chest, and sightless eyes closed. He had been scrubbed clean and shaved, and they had put on his one suit of store clothes, black of color and seldom used.

Raiford looked down at him and thought bitter thoughts. He had been mean and suspicious and irritating; but he had been a blind old man whom Newt Cragg had murdered and there was no way in which Raiford could avenge his death. Oh, he could kill Newt; he could put his gun into the pit of Newt's stomach and fire without any qualms whatever. But that would only make Newt a martyr, and folks would lament his passing and remember what a fine fellow he had been; and Alice Ardell would probably shed tears on his grave.

He turned away and started pacing the room. It was not possible for a man to get away with so much without making a mistake of some kind. Just one tiny loose end was all Raiford needed. It was like a knitted sweater—find one end and pull, and the whole thing came apart. But he couldn't find that end.

He straddled a chair and looked slowly about the room. Tomorrow, after Pop had been properly laid away, Newt would come in here with the deed to the Box L all ready for signing. And he would have to sign it. Newt would gloat and mock him; he might even boast about what he had accomplished. That was a weakness with some clever plotters; they just couldn't help bragging when they thought everything was under control. They could be as slick as a willow whistle about the actual deed, and then risk spoiling the whole thing by talking about it and being overheard.

Raiford jerked himself upright as though the chair had suddenly acquired a charge of high-tension electricity. Overheard. *Overheard!* That was it! That was the way!

He sprang to his feet, his gaze going to the three-foot-square trap door in the ceiling. That was it! But he needed help. Hurd! Hurd was his man.

He was tense in every muscle, his cheeks hot and his eyes glinting. He had to force his face into a mask of inscrutability before he dared leave the house. When he gained control of his emotions he went down to the bunkhouse and called Hurd aside.

"Come up to the house," he said. "Want to talk to you about the funeral."

He led the way into the cabin, waved Hurd into a chair on one side of the table and straddled the one on the other side. He said, "Hurd, I've sized you up as a square shooter. I need somebody to help me and I picked you."

"Want me to rub out Trotter?" asked the little man with the stony face. "It'd be a pleasure!"

"No, not Trotter. I want you to help me rub out somebody else in a real honest-to-goodness legal manner."

"Who?"

"Newt Cragg."

Hurd didn't even blink. "That'd give me even greater pleasure."

"I've got to tell the whole story so that you can realize what the skunk's done and is planning to do. I saw him in town this morning and he told me that he's decided to buy the Box L."

"You ain't crazy enough to sell, are you?"

"I'll probably sell, but I'm not that crazy. Listen."

He started with the night when he had buried James Lanier and then resurrected him, and continued with the story up to the present time. Hurd listened with the same stony expression on his face, but his eyes were glinting with interest.

"So you ain't Jim Lanier after all," he said when Joe had finished.

"I never had any intention of becoming James Lanier; but in Calixto that day Alice Ardell thought she recognized me and I took Lanier's place in order to stop a shoot-out between Trotter and Mel Thorne. Then I had to keep up the bluff until I could talk to Pop. I figured he wouldn't be fooled for a minute, but when I got here Trotter said I was Jim Lanier and Newt Cragg introduced me to Pop as his son. And Pop didn't know the difference because his son had been gone twelve years and Pop was blind."

"Why didn't you tell him after Newt left?"

"Because by that time I realized that somebody was taking advantage of a blind man and his wounded son. I wanted to find out Newt's game, and the first thing I knew I was in it so deep that I couldn't get out."

"But now you figure that Newt pushed Pop off that cliff?"

"Of course. He had to. I thought at first that Newt was ringing in a false son merely to strip the Box L, with the blame falling on the Double A. It wasn't until after Ardell's death that I tumbled to the real scheme. He wanted a son here to buy the ranch from after Pop had met with his 'accident.' The fire was his first attempt to do away with Pop. I came home before he expected me to, otherwise it would have succeeded."

"And you figger he shot Abe Ardell?"

"No. I think the whole idea of starting trouble between the two outfits was to get them to take pot shots at each other. Abe could have been picked off then and his death blamed on a range war. That drive I told you about sort of speeded the thing up. It wasn't Newt who shot Ardell; it was one of his hired men named Squat Armstrong. That was an accident, but it made the range war unnecessary."

"But he still had to get Pop."

"Yes. And he had to get him himself. For one thing he ran no chances; Pop was blind. You don't have to be a gunman to shoot a blind man, and if he can't see it's easy enough to push him over a cliff."

"I'm wonderin'," said Hurd, "why he actually looked up the real son."

"Because if the real son showed up someday and proved his identity, Newt couldn't keep the ranch that had been sold to him by an impostor. He had to get the boy down here and then have Squat Armstrong and Miguel Rosas kill him—or try to."

"Why Miguel? It was a one-man job, and lettin' two in on it was just takin' an extra chance." He hurried on apologetically, "I ain't doubtin' you none, but I want to get the whole picture."

"Sure. Well, Squat's from Montana; he'd never seen Jim Lanier. Miguel knew him as a boy and would recognize him if he hadn't changed too much."

"That makes sense. And I reckon Newt paid off Miguel and Squat with cattle they rustled from the Box L."

"Right."

"I get it now. Simple, ain't it? Newt marries Alice and has the Double A; then he buys the Box L from you and owns the whole valley. All for less'n a thousand dollars, countin' what he's had to pay out on the side. The next step—" His jaws clamped shut and his hard gaze was on Raiford.

"Sure. Me. I'm next. The fake son must be removed or Newt faces a future of blackmail. The $500 he pays me for the ranch will probably go to the one who pots me."

"Squat Armstrong, likely. Okay; with you gone that leaves Miguel and Squat and Trotter, huh?"

"Trotter doesn't know what it's all about. He was hired to make trouble between the two spreads. But Newt would get rid of him just the same. After he has the Box L he'll honey up to Alice and get her to throw her crew with his, and together they'll pull a raid on the Circle Cross when Miguel has some wet cattle on hand. In the mix-up he can take care of Miguel and Trotter. He'll get his cattle back and be in more solid than ever with Alice."

"That leaves Squat; and he knows more than anybody except Newt."

"Yes. Squat probably thinks he's sitting pretty, a full partner of the master mind. But Squat is an escaped murderer; when Newt is finished with him he can put a slug in his back and probably collect a reward for doing it."

There was a short silence, then Hurd spoke. "Beats hell, don't it? You know it all: every move Newt's made and every move he plans to make, and still you're hog-tied. You can't prove a thing against him. Right at this moment you can't prove that he knows you're not James Lanier. You can't prove that he got Squat and Miguel to kill Lanier unless you get one of them to say so; and neither of 'em'll talk because it'll stamp them as murderers. You can't prove that he set the fire or that he pushed Pop over the cliff. You know he's guilty as hell, but you can't prove one little thing."

"That's what's been driving me crazy for the past week— how to pin it on him. It came to me today; that's why I said I needed your help. I'm going to get a confession from Newt, and you're going to hear it."

Hurd stared at him. "You funnin'?"

"No. I'm going to try to trap him. That's where you come in. See that trap door up there in the ceiling? It leads to the loft. Tomorrow morning, after the funeral, I want you to get up there and keep quiet. You can't take a chance looking through the trap door; I'll drill a hole right over the table here. You can hear what we say and you can see us.

"I'm going to bring him in here to sign that deed, and when I've signed it I'm going to try to get him to talk. He knows I know all about what he's done, but he figures he has me where I can't say a word without being exposed and accused of Pop's death. He also thinks I won't be around very long to make trouble. So I think he'll talk. My word alone would be worth absolutely nothing against his; but if you overhear what he says and will testify to it in court, we'll have that jasper's hide nailed to the barn door."

For once Raiford saw some expression on Hurd's face. It fairly shone. He thumbed his fist on the table. "By grab, feller, that ought to do it! You drill that hole right away. I'm mighty glad you let me in on the deal. It stinks, and while I ain't no lily-white angel myself, I sure can't stomach a mess like Newt Cragg's cooked up. You can count on me to the limit."

He extended his hand impulsively, and Raiford gripped it.

"There's just one thing that bothers me," said Hurd. "What became of the fake Jim Lanier—the one Newt really hired?"

"I don't know. Newt evidently doesn't know the fellow personally: he wrote a fellow named Jake Rails to pick one suited to the job and send him down. I've been expecting him to turn up any day, and I've wondered what would happen with two fake Laniers on the job."

"Well, if he stays away until after tomorrow mornin' it won't matter. You get Newt talkin' and I'll be lookin' and listenin'." Hurd's joyous expression changed to one of anxiety. "Say! That feller's slick and he has covered up mighty well; do you think we can swing it?"

"With the help of the real James Lanier, there's no doubt

of it. As soon as I sign the deed I'll make tracks to the ranch where I left him. He should be able to get around by this time. I'll fetch him down, get in touch with you, and the three of us will go to the county seat and tell our story to the law. We'll have Newt hog-tied before he even knows he's been thrown."

"It sure sounds foolproof; I don't see how we can miss." Hurd got up. "You get busy and drill that hole, and tomorrow I'll slip in the house right after the funeral and get set. If you see a chair right under that trap door you'll know I'm up there."

Raiford nodded and Hurd went out. For the first time in days Joe felt relaxed and confident. He had found the answer to his problem and, as Hurd had said, he didn't see how they could miss. All he had to do was to get Newt to talk.

The funeral of Pop Lanier was not nearly so impressive as was that of Abe Ardell. Besides Raiford and the crew there were present only the preacher, Trotter, Newt Cragg and Alice Ardell.

Trotter had ridden out with Newt, and Newt had explained to Raiford.

"He knew Pop; and besides I hired him after you fired him. I'll be taking over right after the funeral and he'll be my new foreman."

Alice rode over just as the service was about to start. Raiford met her, took her extended hand and looked soberly into her eyes which gazed sadly down at him.

"I'm terribly sorry, Jim," she told him.

He murmured his thanks and felt heartily ashamed of himself. He was deceiving this honest girl and he didn't like it a bit. One of the crew took her horse and she walked with him to the grave for the short service.

The Box L men tried to appear sober and impressed, but they were wondering how long it would be before they could get back to their poker game. Raiford assumed an expression suited to the occasion, and Newt Cragg was the picture of reverent sympathy. When it was over Newt said,

"I'll see Miss Ardell home, Jim, and then come back for that little business session we've planned."

Raiford nodded his agreement and said good-bye to Alice. Newt's leaving at this time was really a break for him; during his absence Hurd could be established in the loft.

It was not difficult to manage; Hurd slipped into the cabin without being observed by any of the crew, and Raiford helped him through the opening in the ceiling. Hurd found the hole which had been drilled in the loft floor and Raiford moved the table and chairs slightly so that Newt would be within range of his vision. There must be no mistake; Hurd must be able to swear to Newt's identity by sight as well as by the sound of his voice.

"It's as dusty as all get out up here," came Hurd's muffled voice. "And I got a clean shirt on, too."

"I'll buy you a new silk one with part of Newt's $500," promised Joe.

It was close to noon when Newt returned. Raiford was sitting in Pop's chair on the porch and Cragg dismounted and nodded towards the open door.

"We'll go in and get this over with," he said.

Raiford shrugged and tried to look sullen. He got up and led the way inside, taking the chair he had previously selected and waving Newt to the one on the other side of the table. The lawyer drew a document from his pocket.

"It won't take long. All you have to do is sign on the dotted line. I'll have Trotter witness your signature. The amount named is one dollar and other valuable consideration. That means $500."

"I've been thinking it over," said Raiford. "The job's worth a lot more than that."

"You're getting a lot more than that," Newt told him coldly. "You're escaping conviction for the murder of Pop Lanier."

"You know I didn't kill Pop."

"I can prove that you did."

"Only by exposing me as a fake. How will you go about that?"

"Quite easily. I had some correspondence with James Lanier and his signature is in my possession. Of course, when Alice recognized you instantly I became a bit careless; I didn't check as carefully as I should have. But when your father met with his fatal accident, and you immediately offered to sell the Box L cheap, I became suspicious, I compared your signature on the deed with the signature on James Lanier's letters. I was astounded to find that they were not at all similar. I'm sure you can follow the rest quite easily, clear up to the hangman's noose."

Jim shook his head and tried to appear crestfallen. "I guess you got me hooked. But look what you're getting for $500—a ranch worth $20,000."

A wolfish grin appeared on Newt's face. "Don't forget the Double A. I'll be quite a cattleman when I get through."

"Some fellows have all the luck," sighed Raiford. "Let's see the color of those five hundred bucks."

"Just as soon as I see a sample of your penmanship at the bottom of this document," answered Newt as he slid the paper across the table.

Raiford had pen and ink handy. He wrote James Lanier's

name in the proper place, then looked up quickly at Newt.

"Suppose the real James Lanier shows up? Hadn't counted on that, had you?"

Newt smiled a superior smile. "My boy, I'm not in the habit of overlooking things. You should know that. I told you he'll never show up."

"How do you know? Just because he's been away for twelve years is no sign that he'll never come back. If you were as smart as you think you are you would have let him start back, then lie in the bushes along the trail and pot him before he got here."

"What do you think I did?"

"I don't think you did that," said Raiford promptly. "For one thing you didn't know this Jim Lanier; you couldn't be sure you were rubbing out the right man."

Newt studied him with slightly narrowed eyes. His cleverness was not being properly appreciated and he didn't like that. No harm in telling the fellow as long as there were no witnesses to the conversation present. And Squat Armstrong was laying for him on the trail to Calixto. Squat had his instructions; Squat would follow him at a discreet distance and when he was safely away from the neighborhood of Calixto Squat would deal with him.

Newt got up and walked to the front door. He looked out, came back into the room, looked out of the window and then opened the back door and looked through it, too. He came back and sat down. Raiford was watching him, curiosity and skepticism in his eyes.

"A smart man," said Newt impressively, "never takes chances by doing his own dirty work. It is enough that he furnishes the brains; there are always menials to supply the brawn."

Raiford pretended quick understanding. "Miguel Rosas! You hired him to do it. He knew Lanier when he was a boy."

"You're getting warm," admitted Newt, "but you're still off the trail. Miguel is impulsive, erratic, and a bit too smart to be completely loyal. I hired Miguel to do the spotting; the actual work was done by another, a man without brains or imagination and one who seldom misses what he shoots at."

"I see. But you left yourself wide open, Mr. Smarty. That fellow's going to be in your hair the rest of your life. He'll blackmail you out of every cent you get out of the deal."

Newt smiled confidently. "Don't bother your curly head about that. You know enough to be in my hair for the rest of my days also, but I've got you so sewed up that you dare not try it. Money is very nice to have, if you have enough of it; but all the money in the world is valueless to a man whose neck has been stretched at the end of a rope."

Raiford slumped in his chair and scowled gloomily at the table.

"Yeah, I guess you're right. That five hundred bucks begins to look bigger and bigger. Suppose you hand it over."

Newt drew a roll of bills from his pocket and pushed it across the table. "There it is; count it if you have any doubts."

Raiford counted it and put it carefully into a pocket.

"You killed Pop, of course," he said matter-of-factly. "And Abe Ardell."

"Not Abe. I'd hoped somebody would get him in a cattle war, but the drive speeded things up for me. Pop? Certainly. It was too important to trust to somebody without brains."

There it was, right from the mouth of the man himself! Raiford tried to hide his exultation. He had Newt Cragg right where he wanted him.

And then there came the slightest of scraping sounds from the loft above, and Raiford to his dismay saw a fine trickle of dust filter through the hole and drift down towards the table. To cover the sound and to distract Newt's attention he got quickly to his feet, pushing his chair back noisily.

"I'm on my way," he said tersely. "I've had enough of this place."

"The sooner the better," said Newt, and got up also. "I want immediate possession. I'll go out to the bunkhouse and have Trotter sign this as a witness."

They went out together, Newt to the bunkhouse, Raiford to the corral. The sweat stood out on his forehead as he caught his horse and saddled him. It had been a close call back there, but Newt had not noticed either the sound or the dust.

His horse was still a little lame, but there was no particular hurry. All Raiford had to do now was to get James Lanier, pick up Hurd on the way back, and go to the county seat. He finished saddling and led his horse to the cabin, leaving him standing while he went inside for his bed roll. Newt was still in the bunkhouse with the crew.

He whispered, "Hurd!"

Hurd's face appeared at the edge of the opening. His eyes were shining.

"I got it! Every word! Feller, we got that polecat nailed to the mast!"

"I was afraid you'd given away the whole play."

"It was the dust. I had to tie myself in a knot to keep from sneezin'."

"I'm on my way to get Lanier. You lie low up there until you're sure nobody's around. Trotter will probably fire you. Hang around Calixto until I get back. It'll be four, maybe five days. So long, feller—and thanks!"

14

MINDFUL that he was probably next on Newt's list of victims, Raiford rode with his eyes open and his rifle across his knees. The country between the Box L and Calixto was comparatively open, and anybody taking a shot at him would have to do so from a distance. He glanced back towards the ranch from time to time, but it was not until he had put the forks a mile or so behind him that he noticed he was being followed. The horseman was too far away for positive identification, but he assumed that it was Squat Armstrong.

But nothing happened on the way to Calixto, and while Raiford traveled at a slow pace the horseman did not make any attempt to shorten the distance between them. Raiford left his horse at the Royal Flush, then walked back to the store and entered it. He was watching when Squat rode slowly into town, looking closely at the horses along the street. He must have spotted Raiford's animal outside the Royal Flush, for Joe, watching from the store, saw him turn abruptly into the passageway beside Newt Cragg's office. There, he was sure, Squat would hide until he hit the trail again.

Raiford bought some saddle rations and carried them down the street, watching warily as he passed Newt's office. No doubt Squat had recognized him as Montana Joe, and there was always the danger that he would throw discretion to the winds in an effort to do away with the man he had promised to get. Joe stowed the food in his saddle pockets and went to the restaurant for something to eat, and as he ate he laid his plans.

When he had finished he mounted his horse and set out, not towards the north, but to the west, taking a road he had never traveled before but which he knew ran to the county seat. When he had gone about a mile he looked back from the top of a rise and saw Squat following him at what Armstrong thought was a safe distance.

The trail entered a gap between two ranges of hills and began a winding course which Raiford felt sure would continue until the next valley was reached. This was what he had expected and had been looking for. He turned his horse from the road and pushed him back into the thick growth which fringed the base of a hill. He halted the animal behind a clump of trees, dismounted and stood at the head of the animal. Ten minutes passed and then he heard the thud of hoofs and glimpsed his pursuer as he loped his horse along the trail, heading for the next bend, half a mile ahead. Raiford led his horse to the edge of the brush and watched until Squat had safely rounded the curve, then mounted and cut back in the direction from whence he had come.

He ran his horse now, getting the best speed he could from the still slightly lame animal, and when Calixto came into view he again left the road and headed northeast so as to avoid the town. He came finally to the trail which led northward. He continued along this trail until dusk overtook him. There had been no further sign of Squat.

He camped in a hollow near a spring, some distance from the road, and allowed his horse to graze while he prepared and ate a frugal meal. He smoked a cigarette and loafed until it was dark, then mounted and continued northward. Squat, he felt sure, would ride slowly, watching for his campfire.

He rode all night, camped for an hour in the morning, then continued until noon, when he came to the small ranch where he had left James Lanier to recover from his wound. The rancher was doing his noon chores and came to meet Raiford as the latter dismounted.

They shook hands and Raiford asked, "How's the patient? Well enough to travel yet?"

"I reckon he is. He pulled out yesterday."

The news jolted Raiford. "Left? For Calixto?"

"I reckon so. He didn't say. Borrowed a hoss and rig from me and said he'd either return 'em or send me the money for 'em. You come from Calixto?"

"Yes."

"Funny you didn't pass him on the trail."

"I rode all night; he was probably bedded down somewhere."

He stood thinking it over, alarm for the young man's safety stirring within him. If James Lanier went directly to Newt Cragg, as the chances were he would, his life wasn't worth a plugged nickel. Newt Cragg had the ranch; there was no place in his scheme for the real James Lanier.

Raiford turned to the rancher. "I've got to get back as quickly as I can. My horse is tired and a little lame; have you one I could borrow?"

"Sure. But you'd better come in and eat somethin' first."

"Thanks, but I can't. I haven't the time. I've got to try to catch young Lanier just as soon as I possibly can."

"Well, you know best; but a hundred and forty miles of straight ridin' ain't my idea of fun."

The rancher got a horse for him and turned Raiford's animal into a corral. Joe thanked the man for his kindness and set out again for Calixto.

The worry he felt was all for young Lanier; his case against Newt Cragg would not be weakened very much by the loss of Pop's son. Hurd had the testimony which, when added to his own, would convict the lawyer in any court in the land. The rancher he had just left could testify to the young man's identity and wounded condition. If Newt did away with Lanier there would be just one more murder chalked up against him. But Raiford was determined to save the young man if it were at all possible.

He rode rapidly until dark, camped and prepared his supper, then turned in for a night's sleep. Lanier had a full day's start on him and he could not hope to overtake the fellow even if he rode all night. Two nights in the saddle in succession would only exhaust him and dull his wits at a time when he would need every ounce of his strength and an alert brain. He was up at dawn and on his way again, and sighted Calixto as dusk was shrouding the town.

It was essential that he stop in the town to make inquiries of Lanier, and he realized that this would be a delicate proposition. If Lanier had ridden boldly into town and had announced his identity and produced evidence to back up his claim, then Raiford had been branded as an impostor and would be subject to arrest. If, on the other hand, Newt had disposed of Lanier before he could make his identity known, Raiford ran the risk of death at the hands of Squat Armstrong who, having lost his man, might still be skulking around Calixto.

The shadows were thickening when he rode down the main street but it was still light enough for instant identification. He caught no sight of Squat or of his horse, and headed for the office of the town marshal whose business it was to know if any strangers had hit town. He didn't get the chance to inquire; even as he halted before the office the marshal came running out. His eyes were popping and he had a gun in his hand.

He yelled, "Get your hands up! You're under arrest for the murder of Pop Lanier!"

A swift jerk on the rein, a jab of the spurs, and the tired horse acquired new energy. A startled leap to the left and it settled into a surging run that took it along the dusty street like a flash of light. Joe bent low in the saddle.

Behind him Raiford heard the roar of the marshal's gun, and slugs whistled past him with an ominous hum; but the dust kicked up by flying hoofs formed a screen and he was not hit. The doors of the Royal Flush burst open as he passed and men erupting from the saloon sped him on his way with more hot lead. They fired with more enthusiasm than accuracy though, and he ran the gauntlet unharmed.

Once safely out of town he pulled down to a more sedate pace and sat erect in the saddle. He was sweating, and he mopped his face with his scarf. Newt had lost no time in declaring open season for him. Squat had probably reported his failure and the lawyer had, directly or indirectly, branded him as the killer of Pop Lanier. Raiford no longer had only

Squat to deal with; the gun of every man in or near Calixto would be turned against him.

His face hardened and he set his jaws. It would be only a matter of time before that was rectified. He'd pick up Hurd and together they would ride to the county seat with their stories. The law would take over then. Newt Cragg had reached the end of his rope.

Darkness had fallen by the time he reached the Box L, and he approached cautiously, knowing that here his danger would be greatest. There were lights in both the bunkhouse and the cabin which he assumed had been taken over by Newt Cragg. For the moment he had no interest in Cragg; it was Hurd he had to find. He dismounted and led his horse to the bunkhouse, taking care to make no noise. Dropping the rein, he moved to the doorway, opened the door and stepped inside.

Three of the crew were playing cards. Another sprawled on his bunk. A quick glance told Raiford that neither Trotter nor Hurd was in the room.

"Sit tight!" ordered Raiford, his gun sweeping up to cover them. "Where's Hurd?"

They stared at him with open mouths, then exchanged furtive glances.

"Talk up. Where's Hurd?"

One of them cleared his throat. "He—ain't here."

"Where is he?"

Again there was silence, and Raiford, a sudden premonition gripping him, took a step forward and jerked his gun in the direction of one of them. "You, Panhandle, answer me! *Where's Hurd?*"

"We planted him yesterday."

"You *what!*"

"Buried him. Now wait!" He jerked his hands into the air at sight of the savage look which came into Raiford's face. "Don't take it out on us! We didn't have nothin' to do with it. It was Trotter that shot him."

"Why?"

"Right after you rode away we heard a shot over at the cabin and went to see what was the matter. Hurd was layin' dead on the floor right under that trap door. Trotter was standin' over him with his gun in his hand. He said Hurd got the drop on him from the loft where he was hidin' but that he ducked and shot the feller."

The whole world was crashing about Raiford's ears. So Newt *had* heard that slight sound Hurd made; he *had* noticed the thin stream of dust filtering from the hole. But, running true to form, he had pretended not to. He had stationed Trotter near the door of the cabin with orders to shoot whoever it was hiding in the loft.

Panhandle was still talking rapidly, earnestly.

"What could we do about it? It was none of our business. Trotter and Hurd had been feudin' ever since they joined the outfit. None of us had any call to take up Hurd's fight. Hell, we didn't even half know him."

For a moment Raiford regarded them, his lips clamped tight, his eyes burning with anger. "Where's Trotter?"

"In the cabin with Newt."

"If you don't want to get hurt, keep out of this."

He made no other threat, but they knew by looking at him that it would be wise to obey. This man was on the prod, crazy mad and as dangerous as a cornered cougar. They made no move to detain him as he backed through the doorway, and even after he had left they remained where they were.

Raiford picked up the rein and led the horse to the cabin. He dropped the leather at the little porch and crossed it quietly. He opened the door, pushed it wide and stepped into the room.

Newt Cragg and Trotter were seated in chairs facing each other, and Trotter had tilted his back against the wall and had hooked a heel over the bottom rung. He was in no position to go into action. Newt was sitting upright, but he knew that if he made the slightest move it would be his last. Both men stared at Joe with jaws sagging in surprise and consternation. Raiford gave the lawyer one quick glance, then his hot gaze transfixed Trotter.

He slipped his gun into its holster and stood, half crouched, with elbows slightly bent and fingers curved. He said, "Get up, Trotter, and start shooting."

"N-now wait a minute!" begged Newt. He seemed to have a frog in his throat.

"Shut up! Trotter, get up and start shooting or I'll plug you like you plugged Hurd."

Trotter slowly and carefully unhooked his heel and gently lowered the chair to the floor. He was not afraid. This damned fool was giving him an even break, and that was all he wanted. His black hair straggled across a forehead that was smooth and untroubled, his sharp black eyes boring into the hot blue ones of Raiford; the muscles which had instinctively tensed at sight of his enemy loosened, the fingers of his right hand itching to clutch the butt of his gun.

Newt said no more. Raiford could achieve nothing by killing him. His quarrel was with Trotter; he was bent only on avenging the death of his friend. It occurred to him that no matter what the result of the shoot-out might be he was the gainer. Trotter must eventually be removed, and if the fake Jim Lanier removed him it would save Newt just that much trouble and expense. As for Raiford, his life was already forfeit. Newt found himself wondering how the fellow had managed to evade Squat. Had he in some way bested the stocky gunman Newt had set on his trail? For, contrary to Raiford's belief, Squat had not yet reported to Newt.

All this passed through the lawyer's keen mind while Trotter prepared for what must come. His thoughts were interrupted when Raiford snapped,

"Hurry it up!"

What happened then was too swift for even the observant Newt Cragg to follow accurately. He saw Trotter come out of the chair with amazing speed for a man of his bulk, and when he stood, crouched, the gun was in his hand and roaring. And as he fired, he threw himself to one side and went down, left arm breaking his fall, still firing.

Newt had no time to glance at Raiford, but it seemed to him that the man surely could not match that fast draw and lightning shot; yet he could hear the crash of the gun at his left and when he finally bent a swift look in that direction he saw that Raiford was still on his feet, his set face framed by the blue smoke from his flaming gun.

Newt stared with fascination as Raiford's gun moved slightly and roared again; then he saw the muzzle drop as the bent figure rose. He saw Raiford flip the cylinder of his gun outward and calmly punch four empty shells from it. They dropped to the bare floor with a clatter, and while Newt still stared Raiford punched fresh ones in their places.

Newt turned his head again to look at Trotter. The big man no longer supported himself with his left arm; he had at first fallen on his side and then rolled over on his back. There was a small black hole squarely between his eyes.

It suddenly occurred to Newt that it might be his turn now, and the thought froze the blood in his veins. He thought fleetingly of the gun in its clip holster beneath his arm, but he knew that an attempt to draw it would be the same as committing suicide. Maybe he could talk his way out. He opened his lips but no sound came from them.

Raiford turned his gaze upon him now. He stood there contemplating Newt for a full half minute, the desire to kill still in his eyes. Again Newt opened his mouth and again there came no sound. The sweat gathered on his forehead. Then he saw the fire in Raiford's eyes die, saw an almost imperceptible smile of scorn curve his lips.

"That," came the level voice, "was Trotter's deserts for killing Hurd. He killed him as he would kill a mad dog, without mercy and when he was helpless. It's the only way he could have killed Hurd. I should have shot him like a sitting duck, but I gave him an even break.

"You've already had your break. You got it when Trotter shot

Hurd. He was up in the loft listening to every word you spoke. But you caught that little noise he made and set Trotter on him. It makes you as guilty of Hurd's death as Trotter and I'd be justified in dropping you this second. But that would make a hero of you and let you out the easy way. I'm not content to do that. When you die it'll be after I've shown you up for the dirty crook you are and pinned the murder of Pop Lanier on you. You'll die at the end of a rope."

It was a long speech, but it was delivered with such repressed emotion that the words fairly gushed from Raiford's mouth.

Newt sat there and stared at him, utterly paralyzed, helpless to speak or to move. He was conscious of a great relief; the man didn't intend to shoot him after all. That, thought Newt, was a mistake; for now he had to get Raiford if he himself wanted to survive.

Raiford still stood there regarding him, and for a few seconds there was utter silence in the room; then, to both of them, there came distinctly the heavy thump of boots on the porch outside.

Raiford was standing to one side of the open doorway and knew he had not been seen; now he stepped noiselessly back against the wall and stood in the shadows waiting with leveled gun. Evidently the man outside could see Newt in the light of the lamp, for he called in a loud voice, "Hey, Newt, what in hell's goin' on in there? What's all the shootin' about?"

Before Newt could answer, Squat Armstrong came rushing into the room. His hand rested on the gun at his side and his gaze was fixed on Newt, who still sat rooted to his chair; then Squat's attention was caught by the body on the floor and he stopped abruptly, his eyes bulging.

"Trotter! Newt, how in hell didja do it?" There was reluctant admiration in his voice.

Newt's eyes were flashing a signal even while his brain was telling him that here was another perfect setup. If not the one, then the other! Squat caught the warning in the glance and whirled to face Raiford.

Off balance, he was in no position to shoot; Raiford was, but didn't. In a flash he knew that he must not kill this man. With Hurd gone, his only hope of pinning the guilt on Newt lay in Squat Armstrong. By killing Squat he would only be doing the lawyer a favor.

Stepping forward, he feinted with his left at Squat's stomach; instinctively Squat pulled both arms in front of him to block the blow. Raiford made a swipe with his gun, and the long steel barrel caught Squat just above the left ear. He grunted and sagged to the floor.

Training the gun on Newt, Raiford backed swiftly through the door and crossed the porch. He leaped to the ground, snatched up the rein, and vaulted into the saddle.

The bunkhouse door was open and he could see the crew grouped in the doorway. He wheeled the horse and sent it lunging around the corner of the cabin and into the shadows beyond.

Strength returned to Newt Cragg. He ran to the porch and yelled an order to the crew. "Get that man! Saddle up and get after him! Shoot him on sight! A hundred dollars to the man who gets him!"

He ran down the steps and towards the bunkhouse, urging them to hurry. When they were catching up their horses, he returned to the cabin. Squat was sitting up, feeling tenderly of his injured skull.

Newt's panic was gone; his confidence returned, and with it came the realization that he still needed this man. He stifled the anger he felt against Squat for failing in his mission.

He said, "Hurt you bad?"

Squat got up, the pain on his face hidden behind the scowl of hatred.

"Naw! I'm all right." He started cursing. "I'll get that guy if it's the last thing I do!"

"You had your chance. How did he get away from you?"

Squat turned angrily towards him. "He wouldn'ta if you'd let me lay in the bushes and pot him while he passed like I wanted to!"

"I didn't want him shot so close to the Box L. I explained that. What happened?"

Squat sat down in the chair recently occupied by Trotter, ignoring the dead man who lay at his feet. He bent over and rested his aching head in his hands.

"I follered him like you said. When he left Calixto he headed west. I kept about a mile behind him. He musta suspicioned me. The trail was windin' and I didn't know he'd ducked until it straightened out. Then I hada push on to make sure he'd doubled back. I went back to Calixto and asked for him. Nobody'd seen him come back into town. I rode north damned near fifty miles before I give it up and turned back. In Calixto they said he'd just showed up again but that he left with a flock of bullets around him. I didn't figger he'd head out here, but I come on to report. What happened?"

Newt told him. "You've got to get him now."

"You tellin' me? You shore picked a dandy for your fake Jim Lanier! You picked a lawman! He's the feller that's after me—Montana Joe!"

It was Newt's turn to stare.

15

RAIFORD STRUCK OUT along the road which led to the forks and Calixto, but he did not keep to it. The hunt was on; Newt would give his men no rest until they had removed for all time this one man who stood between him and the complete realization of his ambitions. He had confirmed the brand of murderer they had put on him by the killing of Trotter; trust Newt Cragg to distort the facts in the case to his own advantage.

When he had ridden until he thought it safe to do so, he left the trail and cut due northward, crossing the Box L range some distance from the buildings and then circling to the path which led up the slope to the Circle Cross. He was glad now that his previous excursions had made him familiar with the rugged terrain, and that darkness would prevent any spotting from the peak.

When he came to the fissure in the rock where he had first encountered Squat Armstrong, he turned into it and found his way to the basin. In it he found a grassy place for his horse and staked it out; then he dragged his saddle and blankets to a nest of rocks where, because of the loose stone underfoot, no one could approach without giving him warning. Here he made his bed.

He lounged on his blankets smoking and grimly contemplating the succession of events that had demolished all his carefully thought out plans for the undoing of Newt Cragg. He had counted on James Lanier at least for the nullifying of the grab of the Box L, and now the fellow had disappeared. He had been certain that Hurd's testimony would utterly condemn Newt Cragg, and now Hurd was gone. Instead of holding the whip hand he was a fugitive, accused of the murder of Pop Lanier and Trotter, and, possibly, of Abe Ardell.

There was no one to whom he could possibly look for help. Alice Ardell had promised him her trust and confidence, but could she continue to believe in him after Newt had presented the mass of so-called evidence against him? He doubted it. But if everything else failed he must put her loyalty to the test.

He was concerned with the whereabouts of young Lanier. The boy would naturally return to Calixto and make at once for the Box L. He might have already done so and met the fate which had overtaken his father. Certainly he wouldn't head for any other place unless—

A startling thought came to Raiford. Suppose—just suppose—that this man who had been wounded was not James Lanier but the man who had been sent by Jake Rails to take Lanier's place! In that case the attack on him by Squat and Miguel may have scared him so badly that as soon as he was able to travel he had lost no time in getting away from that part of the country.

Raiford thought this over and finally arrived at a dead end. In that case the real James Lanier was still roaming around somewhere. Also it would mean that Miguel, who had been selected to accompany Squat because he could identify Lanier, had made a mistake in his man.

Raiford finally gave it up and went to sleep.

He spent the whole of the next day resting his horse and himself and trying to map out some sort of campaign. The whole thing resolved itself into this: he must capture Squat and through him or Miguel reach the truth about Newt Cragg. He could not go directly to Miguel because the Mexican had let him down when he attempted to prove his alibi at the time of Pop's death and might conceivably take him prisoner or even shoot him to forward his own plans. His food was gone, and he must have help. He must try to see Alice Ardell.

It was fairly late when he emerged upon the range, and he lost no time in crossing to the Double A side of the fence. The moon had risen, and he kept to the low spots as much as possible as he worked his way southward. He was taking a big chance, for he knew that Newt would probably have both crews searching for him and could only hope that they would confine their looking to the daylight hours. This, he soon learned, was a vain hope.

He was crossing the same ridge where the attack on the rustlers had taken place when a voice suddenly challenged, "Pull up, there!"

Instantly he bent low and fed his horse the spurs. Guns roared as he sped down the slope and lead whined about his ears. His horse hit the creek at full speed and water flew in sheets as the animal lunged across the ford. He angled up the other slope, bearing westward in the direction of the fence. He knew he would have no time to cut wire, but by following it to the valley road there was a chance that he could get through the gate and to the Box L side. Then, by doubling back, he might reach the sanctuary of the hills.

Crossing the ridge was the dangerous part of it, and he stooped even lower as he neared the top. They were close on his heels and their guns spoke again as he flashed over the summit. He felt a solid blow on his left shoulder, followed by a searing pain. They kept firing, and his horse squealed and made a frantic bound that nearly unseated Raiford. The horse had been hit, too. He could not turn without losing ground; his only hope lay in reaching the road.

He caught sight of it at last, a yellow streak beneath the rays of the moon, and he turned still more to the west so as to strike it at the point where it was crossed by the fence. His glance swept along it and over towards the Box L range. He knew then that this way of escape was also denied him, for he could see a band of horsemen galloping rapidly along the road and headed for the gate. The Box L crew was abroad too and, hearing the shots, were closing in for the kill.

He could not keep on to the western hills; even if his horse lasted, the Box L men would turn with him and the Double A men would swing off to his left and he would be exposed to a murderous crossfire. His only possible chance lay in trying to cut across the front of the Double A men and heading south through the middle of the valley. Although he had never been farther than the Double A ranch, he knew that beyond it lay more hills. He swung the horse sharply to the left and raked it with steel.

It was close. Once more the guns crashed out and the only thing that saved him was the fact that the marksmen were firing from the backs of galloping horses. Had one of them thought to pull up and take deliberate aim he would have been tumbled from his saddle; but they were wrapped up in the excitement of the chase and would not check their speed. As it was, he swept ahead of the foremost rider by a narrow margin. Ahead of him, and a bit to his right, he caught a gleam of light from the Double A ranch house and headed directly for it.

And now his horse began to falter. It was breathing in great gasps and its muscles were moving spasmodically. He kept it going somehow, still heading for the lighted house. It seemed an eternity before the Double A buildings loomed up before him.

The house faced the east and its back was in shadow; he guided his flagging mount into the gloom, dropped quickly to the ground and gave the animal a whack to keep it going. He had just time enough to throw himself flat beside the kitchen steps when the pursuing horsemen thundered by.

The back door opened and a shaft of light made him hug the earth. He heard a low, tremulous whisper, "Jim!"

He raised his head and saw Alice Ardell outlined in the kitchen light.

"Yes." There was nothing else he could say. If she called to Mel Thorne he was lost.

"Wait!" She ran into the kitchen and extinguished the light. He couldn't see her now, but he heard her feet on the steps, then felt her hand touch his wounded shoulder. Involuntarily he shrank back.

"You're hurt!"

"Not badly."

"Give me your hand—quick!"

His heart leaped; she was not going to betray him. He grasped her hand and got to his feet. Her arm went about him, steadying him. From the north came the roll of hoofs which told of the approach of the Box L crew. From beyond the house to the south there sounded yells and commands. He heard Mel Thorne call, "I found his horse! He's afoot somewhere! Spread out, you fellers, and if you spot him let him have it!"

"Hurry!"

She helped him up the steps and through the doorway. She

107

shut and barred the door behind them, then got to her knees and started unbuckling his spurs.

"I'm not that helpless," he whispered.

"Sh-h-h! We mustn't let Mother hear."

She put the spurs on a table and led him into the living room, both of them treading like stalking cats, then through another doorway and into a room that he knew from its fragrance must be hers. She turned him and he felt his legs strike the soft edge of a bed.

"Sit down," she whispered and pushed gently. "Try not to make a sound."

"I'll get your bed all mussed up," he objected.

"It doesn't matter. Please be quiet."

Her hand was on his shoulder, and he felt her tense as the soft tread of feet sounded outside the door.

"Alice!" came a low-pitched voice.

"Yes, mother?"

"Is that Jim Lanier with you?"

He heard her catch her breath. Then she crossed swiftly to the door and opened it. "Yes, it is, Mother. Oh, please—!" Her voice caught. "He's hurt," she finished simply.

"Light the kitchen lamp and pull down the shades. You'd better bar the front door, too. I'll heat water and get some bandages."

Alice gave a little exclamation of relief, and Raiford relaxed his taut muscles. This woman whom he had never met before was certainly one of God's own people!

She came into the room, closed the door and moved to the window. She drew down the shades and pulled the curtains together, then lighted a lamp. Turning the wick low, she straightened and looked at the wounded man.

She was a plump little woman, motherly appearing and capable; but a life on the frontier had endowed her with patience and courage and tolerance. No matter what this man had done, he was in need of medical attention in a land where doctors were few and far between; and she would attend to his wounds first, even if she must turn him over to be hanged later.

Raiford could hear horsemen riding about the house, probing into the shadows, looking every place where the fugitive might be concealed. He heard the front door rattle and heard Alice call, "Who is it?"

"It's Mel," came the muffled answer. "Keep the house locked up, Alice. Lanier's on the loose and he's desperate!"

A wry grin twisted Raiford's mouth. "Do I look desperate?" he asked.

He thought the grave eyes twinkled just a bit. "You certainly don't act like it."

Alice came in, a tight smile on her pale lips, and Mrs. Ardell went to the kitchen for water and bandages. While she was gone, Alice helped Raiford off with his coat, then skillfully cut away the shirt around the wound. The bullet had raked across the shoulder blade, gouging a groove in the flesh but not breaking the bone. Mrs. Ardell came in and he straddled a chair so that they could cleanse the wound and bind a compress in place.

"I'll talk while you work," Raiford said softly. "But I wish you'd tell me first just what you've heard about me."

"We heard," said Mrs. Ardell tightly, "that you shot my husband and then pushed Pop Lanier off the cliff to his death. Your own father."

"And that you m-murdered that man, Trotter," added the girl. "Newt Cragg told you?"

"Yes. He said there was no doubt about your killing Pop. You were riding the horse with the broken shoe, weren't you?"

"Yes. But not on the day Pop was killed."

"He mentioned that, too," said Alice in a flat voice. "But he explained that you could have switched horses. There was nobody on the ranch to see you."

"Did he explain why, after I'd gone to the trouble to switch horses, I'd pick the same one to ride on the very day we found Pop?"

"No, he didn't," said Mrs. Ardell shortly. "And we both wondered about it. It seemed such a crazy thing to do."

Alice observed him gravely. "It was the one thing that made us doubt. That, and what you told me that day in the hills. I could believe that you shot Trotter; he was a horrid man and did his best to force our boys into a fight that day at Calixto. I'd never blame you for shooting Trotter. But Newt made it sound like wanton murder. He said you shot Trotter before he could get out of his chair."

"And didn't you wonder," asked Raiford gently, "why such a hardened killer would let Newt live to tell the story?"

"He said that one of the crew walked in on you and that you had to run."

Raiford smiled grimly. "A reason for everything, eh? That's the legal mind for you. One of his men did walk in on us, but it wasn't a Box L man. It was Squat Armstrong, the man I told you killed Mr. Ardell."

Mrs. Ardell straightened suddenly. "How do you know that?" she asked sharply.

"Because I was there and saw him. Saw him and couldn't do a thing about it. Mrs. Ardell, I had a talk with Alice right after Mr. Ardell's death, but I didn't take her entirely into my confidence. Now I'm going to put my cards on the table. It's the showdown, and I need your help. To begin at scratch, I'm not James Lanier. My name is Joe Raiford. In Montana they call me Montana Joe. I was a marshal up there."

Alice gave a gasp of surprise and stepped back a pace. In

the dim light Raiford could see her eyes, wide and startled and with a bit of horror in them.

"Not—Jim Lanier?"

"No. As I told you, I was a marshal up in Montana. I was on my way south in search of a little cow spread where I could settle down and forget the danger and bloodletting; but one night while I was lying by my campfire—"

He went on to tell the rest of the story, and by the time he had related how he had saved the young man's life, he sensed the swing of their sympathy in his direction. Concisely he related for them the events which followed: his acceptance by Pop Lanier; the arrogant manner of Newt Cragg which had so aroused his anger and suspicion; the finding of the hideout in the north hills and his meeting with Squat; the shooting of Ardell and his inability to accuse Squat without being exposed as an impostor and having the killing fastened on himself; and finally his version of the death of Pop Lanier while he was in the hills, and Newt's subsequent demand that he sell the Box L for $500.

There was a long silence while the two women stood regarding him and he sat quietly on the chair and waited for the full significance of what he had told them to sink in. Finally Alice said in a strained voice, "Then Newt knew the whole time that you were not really James Lanier."

"Of course. He wanted someone here who could pass as Lanier's son in order that he could 'buy' the Box L after Pop had been eliminated. But he didn't want the real son to show up after the transaction had been completed, so he had a friend send down a man who could claim to be James Lanier. Then he hired Squat Armstrong and Miguel to waylay the real son and dispose of him."

"And where," asked Mrs. Ardell, "is the man who was hired to take Jim Lanier's place?"

"That's one thing that I don't know. I can only guess. If he showed up after I had been proclaimed Pop's son, Newt might have paid him off and sent him home, figuring that if he denounced me as an impostor he'd have trouble passing off another man as Pop's son. Newt knew that whoever I was he had me sewed up. All he had to do was denounce me as an impostor to discredit any story I might tell.

"There's another theory, but it's rather a farfetched one. Squat and the Mexican might have waylaid the wrong man and shot the substitute instead of the real Lanier. But that doesn't help, for in that case the real son is alive and should have shown up long ago."

"The thing to do," said Mrs. Ardell, "is to ride to that ranch where you left the wounded man and question him. You can soon find out if he is the real son or not."

"I did that. I went through the motion of selling the ranch to Newt because I couldn't do anything else and because I knew that the sale was null and void. Then I went after the man. He was gone. He had left the ranch the day before, and should have reached Calixto before I got back. But I don't believe he has, and that is why I thought that he might be the substitute. If he is, he could have been so frightened at his close call that he got out of the country as soon as he could travel."

"It all sounds so logical," said Alice. "But you really haven't a bit of proof, have you? Not one thing to tie these terrible things to Newt Cragg."

"That's right. He's too smart for me. Even when I thought I had him convicted by his own admissions in the presence of a witness, he proved too smart for me."

He told them about the conversation in the cabin with Hurd watching and listening in the loft, and of his finding Hurd dead upon his return, shot by Trotter as he descended from the loft.

"That's why I killed Trotter," he finished quietly. "I gave him every chance; I put my gun in its holster and waited until he got out of his chair. I didn't kill Newt because I want him to be convicted before he dies; and I didn't kill Squat Armstrong because I may be able to get something out of him that will help pin the whole thing on Newt."

Alice was standing stiff and tense, her fists clenched at her sides. She said, "It was Newt who pushed Pop off the cliff. It had to be. He wouldn't dare let anybody else do it."

"That's right. It was one of the things he said that Hurd could have testified to. Newt said it was too important to trust to anybody without brains. He was referring to Squat, I think." He shrugged, then winced at the pain. "He had an alibi that'll be mighty hard to break. He told the bartender and some others in the Royal Flush that he had to ride north about twenty miles to get a paper signed, or something, and he actually started in that direction. Nobody knows who he was supposed to see and it's going to be awfully hard to check up on his movements."

"I suppose so. He's very clever." The tautness went out of her and her slim shoulders drooped. Suddenly she straightened, her eyes brightening with excitement. "But wait! Pop was killed on Friday, wasn't he?"

"Yes. We found him Saturday morning."

Alice spoke to her mother. "What day was it that I rode to Calixto for the mail?"

"Friday afternoon."

"Then I can prove that Newt Cragg did not ride twenty miles north that afternoon! It was between two and three and I was just a mile or so from Calixto when my horse picked up a stone. I pulled off to one side of the road and tried to pry the stone out with a stick. I happened to glance up and saw a man cutting across the range to the east. It was Newt! I remember because I wondered why he hadn't kept to the road. It looked as though he was trying to get to the Box L without being seen."

"Good for you!" said Raiford exultingly. "It doesn't actually pin the murder on him, but it breaks his alibi into small pieces!"

"Now if you can only get Miguel or Squat Armstrong to tell who hired them to kill James Lanier, the rest will be easy."

He smiled wryly. "Anything will be easy compared with that. Squat is under sentence to hang for another murder; talking won't help him. It all seems to rest with Miguel. If Squat did the actual shooting, or if I can convince Miguel that they did not kill their man, he might talk. He doesn't like either Squat or Newt. He seems to have some plan of his own to put Newt in his place. Said he had an ace in the hole."

He stopped abruptly, his eyes narrowing. "We might have something there! What is it that Miguel knows about Newt? What is this ace in the hole? It might be the very thing we need!"

"You may not be able to make this Squat talk," said Mrs. Ardell, "but Miguel Rosas is a horse of another color. We must get in touch with him at once."

"We'll have to hurry," Alice told them. "When Newt came over today to tell us about your shooting Trotter, he said he'd discovered that it was Miguel who was doing the rustling, running Box L cattle over our range to throw Pop off the trails. He suggested taking both crews and raiding the Circle Cross in the morning. If we find any rustled cattle—"

"You will," interrupted Raiford. "And that'll mean the end of Miguel. He knows too much and must be silenced. And maybe in the mix-up Newt will get his chance to do away with Squat. That will leave only me, and I'm fair game for the first one who gets me in his sights."

Her eyes reflected horror. "What can we do?"

Mrs. Ardell spoke crisply. "We must get word to Miguel at once. He's in it as deep as any, but we've got to save him from the wreckage or let Newt Cragg get away with it. I never did like that shyster."

"We could send Mel," said Alice. "He's hotheaded, but if we tell him the whole story he and the whole crew would be all for Mr. Raiford."

Mrs. Ardell said, "No, we must keep Mel and the crew in the dark for the time being. Newt Cragg is clever; no matter how hard they tried to keep our secret, somebody would give it away. Right now Newt thinks Mr. Raiford is the only one who's onto his game except this Armstrong man whom he plans to eliminate anyway. Let him keep on thinking so until we have the proof we need."

"Then I'll go," said Alice. "I know Miguel; he'll listen to me."

Raiford objected to this. "Your own men would turn you back if they caught you out on the range tonight. If anybody on the Box L intercepted you, Newt would be suspicious at once. We simply can't underestimate him; he's trumped my best cards as fast as I've played them. I'll go myself."

"But you're hurt! And your horse—"

"Mr. Raiford's right," said Mrs. Ardell firmly. "Risky as it is, he must go. Alice, go out and saddle a horse for him. Saddle your own; it's in the barn and you're not so apt to be seen. While you're doing it, I'll fix something for Mr. Raiford to eat."

"My friends call me Joe."

"Very well, Joe. Alice, saddle that horse."

The girl hesitated, her anxious gaze on Raiford; but he smiled at her and got up to show that he was quite himself again, and at last she went out, using the front door and circling the house to see if the way was clear.

He was eating a hasty lunch when she returned.

"It's saddled and ready. I left it in the stable. There's a back door opening directly onto the range. Both crews are riding circle. I think your best plan would be to pretend to be one of them until you get a chance to slip away. And Joe, please take care of yourself."

He got up. "Don't worry, I will. I can't tell you how much your faith has meant to me. I wasn't quite licked, but pretty close to it. Now I know that we're going to scotch the snake that's been spreading its venom on your range. I'll never forget either of you."

Mrs. Ardell smiled at him. "Alice told me that she'd promised to trust you; I'd be a poor mother if I didn't have faith in her judgment. Now we'll put out the light and you can slip out. The stable's right behind the house. Good night, Joe, and good luck."

He pressed her hand and she left the kitchen. Alice blew out the light, then removed the bar from the door and, opening it, stood watching and listening for a few seconds. Then she turned to him and for a short space they stood facing each other in the dark. She put a hand lightly on his sleeve and he knew she was fighting for self-control.

"Good night, Joe," she said at last. "We'll be praying for you."

"Good night, Alice," he said softly.

She moved aside and he went out into the moonlight. He stole across the yard to the darkness of the stable, and he knew that she was still standing in the kitchen doorway watching him. He found the horse and led it from its stall and down the aisle to the open rear door. He got into the saddle and walked the horse from the yard. He felt strong and confident; he wasn't going to let these two noble women down.

16

THE MOON WAS HIGH, but at first he saw no rider; then he caught sight of a vague shape to the south and instantly turned his horse in that direction. Whichever crew this man belonged to, he'd think Joe a member of the other if he didn't get a good look at him. Joe held his horse to a slow lope until he was within a hundred feet of where the other waited. The man called to him.

"What you doin' down here? We been all over this territory."

"Thought I seen somethin' to the north," Raiford answered gruffly.

"Well, come on. We're workin' east and west towards the hills. He's afoot and he sure ain't roamin' around over the open range."

He wheeled his horse and set out in a westerly direction. Raiford swung in behind him and remained there until he saw a little depression which would afford him cover. He turned into this and when he emerged on its far side the other rider had vanished. He turned east and headed for the hills and the path which led to the Circle Cross.

It was past midnight when he reached the basin which sheltered Miguel Rosas' headquarters. As he entered it and started down the gentle slope a voice challenged from the shadows and Raiford immediately halted and raised his hands.

"*Quién es?*"

"Jim Lanier. I want to see Miguel at once."

A horseman rode out of the shadows, a rifle held at the ready. "Ride on, *señor*. I'm follow."

Raiford rode slowly down the slope and across the basin, halting before the shack where he had eaten with Miguel. The Mexican called out in Spanish and Miguel came out of the doorway and into the moonlight.

"Ees the *Señor* Lanier," announced the guard.

Miguel waved him back, and the guard withdrew out of earshot. He kept his rifle pointed at Raiford.

Joe spoke tersely. "Miguel, you gave me a dirty deal when you let Newt Cragg pin the murder of Pop Lanier on me; but now the double-crosser is gunning for you and we've got to stand him off together. At dawn he's coming up here with the Box L and Double A crews to raid you. I reckon Squat Armstrong'll be with him. Got any wet cattle around where he can find them?"

Miguel swore for a full minute, the Spanish words hissing and crackling. Raiford did not understand much Spanish, but he gathered that both Newt and Squat were pigs and the sons of pigs, and that their offspring for many generations would be creatures of unspeakable debasement. He was breathless when he had finished.

"No doubt you're right," said Raiford, "but it seems to me that we ought to get busy moving those cattle. If Newt doesn't find any evidence of rustling for the Double A to see, his hands are tied—I hope."

Miguel got busy. He ran from cabin to cabin pounding on doors, calling excitedly and angrily for his men. They came rushing out, horses were caught and saddled and in a remarkably short time the party was organized. Miguel led them from the basin, Raiford riding beside him. He was quite sure that they suspected him. If this proved to be a trap they would make certain that he was the first to fall into it.

They rode directly to the park where Raiford had found the thirty Box L steers. The animals were bunched, the Mexicans took their stations and the drive started. Raiford rode at point with Miguel, and close behind rode the guard with a rifle. Miguel appeared to be uncertain.

"W'ere we put dem? Thees Strongarm, ees know all the hiding place."

"Drive them down into the valley as fast as you can. You don't want them to be found anywhere near the Circle Cross. Are these all of them?"

"All, señor—w'at ees name?"

"It's supposed to be Lanier."

"Of a certainty! Ees wan good joke on Miguel Rosas. Miguel ees see dis Jeem Lanier many tam before he ron away, and Miguel never forget the face. No matter w'at 'appen, my frien', remember dat. Miguel Rosas never forget the face."

Raiford did not answer. Of course Miguel knew he wasn't James Lanier; was he trying to tell Raiford that he knew the man he and Squat had waylaid was not Lanier either? The crazy idea concerning Miguel's ace in the hole which had seized him in the Double A ranch house returned, and he considered it as they rode.

They finished the job an hour or so before dawn. The stolen cattle were pushed out on the Box L range as far as they dared drive them; then the whole party turned back along the trail to the Circle Cross.

"And now," advised Raiford, "I think it would be a good idea to keep out of Newt's sight."

"She's good idea for you, my frien', but to Miguel Rosas there ees come no 'arm. She's 'onest mans, and the *vaqueros* of the *Señorita* Ardell weel not permit heem to be shoot."

"I wouldn't bank on that. Newt Cragg wants you out of the way—bad."

"Miguel ees not afraid. You mus' not forget hees ace in the 'ole."

"I haven't forgotten. It's what really brought me up here

to see you. I've done you a good turn, Miguel, and one good turn deserves another. What is your ace in the hole?"

"Ees not tam to tell. How I know you do the good turn? Eef Newt Cragg come op weeth the mans, den I know. And den I tell."

There was no use arguing or pleading with him. Nor, Raiford realized, could he force the information from Miguel. He must string along with the Mexican and try to win his confidence. The morning would bring Newt Cragg and then he would know.

He said, "You'll find I played square with you. I'll be around. I'll see you in the morning. Better post guards."

"You come stay weeth me at the *casa*, no?"

"No. I've done all I can for you. It's your fight from here on. If you won't help me, I won't help you. So long."

He turned and rode away into the darkness, leaving Miguel gazing after him. The Mexican swore softly.

"Ees the man. Ees the man who bury the one Strongarm is shoot. Thees peeg Strongarm say he ees man of the law, and he know eet ees Strongarm and Miguel who shoot the one he buries. Am I the fool to tell heem? I'm theenk not!"

He rode away towards the Circle Cross.

Newt Cragg led the party with Squat Armstrong at his side. Behind them were the five Box L men, and the Double A riders under Mel Thorne and Alice brought up the rear. Alice was present on sufferance. They had tried to make her change her mind about accompanying them; but she insisted that she must be one of the party, and they were finally forced to agree.

The course selected by Squat kept them out of sight of the peak, and they crossed the road at a point where a rocky eminence hid them from observation. If all went well they should be able to locate the stolen cattle and take Rosas completely by surprise. So thought all of them but Alice.

Newt was not in a particularly good humor. The failure of the two crews to find and eliminate the one man he feared both puzzled and alarmed him. The fellow had as many lives as a cat. On foot and probably wounded, he had escaped their intensified search. Trotter was gone; Miguel would get his this very day. When Squat had disposed of the Mexican, Newt would dispose of Squat. That would leave nobody but this ex-marshal from Montana. He surely couldn't dodge them forever; the odds against him were too heavy.

It was close to nine o'clock when Squat directed Newt into a passage which wormed its way between two hilly shoulders. "They're in this park," he said. "About thirty of them."

They made an abrupt turn and emerged upon the edge of a grassy basin hemmed in by steep hills. Squat swore throatily and Newt looked at him and said, "Do I need glasses?"

"They was here," said Squat. "They been moved. Come on; they gotta be somewhere around here. Dang it, I helped put them here."

They skirted the edge of the park and found an exit on the far side. After some more careful riding to avoid detection they entered another park. There were cattle here, but search as they would they could find no brand but that of the Circle Cross.

Squat led them to another park—and another disappointment; and thereafter to more parks and more disappointments. His frown became heavier at each stop, and Newt's anger grew by the minute. The Double A men became disgusted and their suspicion of the Box L returned. When noon came and passed without the discovery of any rustled cattle, Mel Thorne, tired after a night of searching for James Lanier, rode up to join Newt and Squat as they regarded still another empty park.

"Our outfit's ridin' back to the Double A," he announced shortly. "Don't look to me like we're ever goin' to find any rustled stock up here."

"They're around somewhere," declared Newt. "They've got to be. Damn it, Mel, there's so many of these places. We'll come across them yet."

"You and your crew can handle it. We're goin' home."

They rode away, but they didn't go home. At Alice's command they pulled off the trail several miles distant and went into camp, staking out their horses and themselves munching saddle rations she had insisted they bring along. She had not confided in Mel; but she knew that Joe Raiford was here in the hills and she wanted to be in a position to help him if he needed help.

Back at the park, Newt said to Squat, "It's rather odd, those wet steers disappearing so suddenly. I'm wondering if your friend Montana Joe had anything to do with it."

Squat scowled. "What could he have to do with it?"

"He got completely away from us last night, didn't he? He couldn't go to Calixto without being blasted out of his boots, and he couldn't hide very well on the open range. He'd been up here before and he knew Miguel. I think we'd better drop in on Miguel's headquarters."

"You won't find no wet cows there."

"We don't need to, now that the Double A is gone."

Squat grunted. "You can go there if you want to; me, I aim to find that Montana lawman and fix his clock oncet and for all."

Newt gave a surly assent and led his men towards the road. Squat rode away in the opposite direction.

Raiford lay on his stomach on the rocks gazing steadily through the field glasses he had found in a shack on the lookout peak. He had been watching since daybreak and had got only an occasional glimpse of Newt and his men. Those few glimpses, however, had shown him that Squat Armstrong was in the party.

Miguel was at the Circle Cross, confident that no harm could come to him as long as the Double A crew rode with Newt. Raiford had his doubts; things had been hanging fire long enough, and Newt knew that he must clean house before matters became too complicated.

Raiford stiffened and adjusted the focus of the glasses. A body of horsemen had emerged on the road which led to the Circle Cross, and there were but six of them. Newt Cragg rode at their head, and Raiford identified the five who followed him as members of the Box L crew. The Double A men were no longer with them, nor was Squat.

He got quickly to his feet, went to his horse and, putting the glasses into a saddle pocket, mounted and headed for Miguel's camp. He had told Rosas that the fight was his own, but he could not let Newt surprise him, and the warning might win Miguel to his side. When he entered the basin the Mexicans had just finished their dinner and were lounging about the buildings. He rode to the main building and called and Miguel came out.

"You better get ready to show that hole card," Raiford told him shortly. "Newt's on his way here with his five men. The Double A crew aren't with him."

Miguel looked startled. "Jus' mans from the Box L? Ees bad!"

"You figure this bunch of yours can stop them?"

Miguel shrugged, frowning. "These are *vaqueros;* they not fight so good. I t'ink we go." He gave some orders in Spanish and the Mexicans ran for their horses. "Come," he said to Raiford, and swung into his saddle. "We go 'nodder way."

They rode through the rear entrance to the *rancho* and presently descended into the basin which contained the log cabin where Raiford had heard that peculiar thump. Its door was closed and a Mexican sat outside with his back to the wall. Miguel waved Raiford to a halt and rode over to the fellow. They talked for a moment or two, then Miguel rejoined Raiford and they continued on their way.

They circled to the west and finally reached a high plateau covered with boulders which appeared to have been strewn by a prodigal Gargantuan hand. Here they halted and Miguel said, "Now we see w'at she's do." He pointed, and Raiford had a distant view of the basin with its buildings. Riding into it he could see six horsemen. He got out the glasses and leveled them, took a look, then handed them to Miguel. The Mexican swore in Spanish.

"They go in my *casa!* One of dem ees get the wood. They are going to burn eet!"

He lowered the glasses and the eyes he turned on Raiford were hot with hate.

"I reckon it's time for us to come to an understanding, Miguel. You can see for yourself what kind of a fellow this Newt Cragg is. Take a good look at me and see if you don't recognize me as somebody you saw by a campfire sixty, seventy miles to the north."

Miguel did not appear to be surprised. He shook his head. "I tol' you Miguel never forget the face. You are Montana lawman; you bury the mans the beeg peeg Strongarm ees shoot."

"That's right. You can talk free, Miguel, for that man did not die. I dug him up after you'd gone and left him with a rancher to get well. The law doesn't want you, but it does want Squat and, most of all, Newt Cragg. Newt hired you and Squat to waylay Lanier and kill him, didn't he?"

"Si! I'm to pick heem out, Squat ees to do the shoot. Me, I'm mak moch noise with the gon, but I miss. I'm not lak to shoot mans een the back."

"You'll testify to that in court? If you do, it'll hang Newt Cragg."

"Si! I'm tell the whole t'ing. I'm tell plenty! An' den I show my 'ole card and Newt's goose she's cook! Ah, the *casa* she's all smoke!"

Raiford took the glasses from him. They had set Miguel's house on fire and were now putting the torch to the other buildings. Newt, failing to find Miguel, was venting his anger in this way.

"That hole card," said Raiford. "What is it?"

But Miguel was dancing with rage. *"Cochino!"* he screamed. "Peeg! Always he treat me, Miguel Rosas, lak the *peon!* But me, I'm *caballero!* And now I'm feex heem with the law! I'm tell everyt'ing and he 'ang by the neck!"

They did not see the horseman who emerged onto the top of a rocky ridge behind them. Squat Armstrong had reached the highest point in that region and now he sat his horse like an Indian sentinel, his keen eyes sweeping the surrounding terrain. They picked out the blazing shacks and the six horsemen, rested momentarily on each exposed spot to the east of his position, then took in his immediate surroundings. Suddenly the bullet head stopped its slow movement and the heavy frame seemed to freeze. His gaze remained fixed, and from his throat came a low growl of triumph. In the next moment he kicked his horse into activity, sending it down the incline and out of the range of vision of the two men he had spotted.

Raiford turned away from the seething Mexican to look apprehensively behind him. An uncanny sixth sense had warned him of danger from that direction. His gaze swept the height which Squat Armstrong had just left, then fixed itself on the huge rock formations which might conceal a hundred enemies.

He turned back to Miguel, who was panting for breath after his vociferous explosion. "I don't like this," he said sharply. "Squat's somewhere on the loose and we're too exposed up here."

"Ees good place," said the Mexican tightly. "I'm 'ope Newt Cragg ees see us and comes. We pick heem off lak the pigeon. Ees t'ousand places we can 'ide."

"That's just what I don't like about it. Others could hide up here, too."

A hundred yards behind them a heavy face peered from the shelter of a rock. A pair of sharp eyes picked out the route to follow, and a bullet head nodded its satisfaction. The face disappeared.

Again Raiford turned as though warned of Squat's approach, but there was nothing to be seen but rocks.

"I'm getting the willies," he murmured. "Miguel, let's get out of this."

"Wait! Dey are leave the *rancho*. We mus' see w'ere dey go."

A hoarse, triumphant shout sounded behind them.

"Gotcha!"

Raiford spun, hand flashing to hip, the quick turn throwing him off balance. He never got the gun to a level. He had one glimpse of Squat Armstrong crouched and with a flaming gun in his hand, then the whole world exploded. He fell over backward, rolled on his right side and lay still.

Miguel wheeled. For an instant he stood with bulging eyes and open mouth; then he uttered a yell of terror and ran for his horse. Squat's gun followed him; its muzzle passed the running body and vomited smoke and flame. Miguel staggered, recovered, stumbled forward. With the grin of a killer on his face, Squat aimed deliberately and fired again. Miguel went to his knees, teetered there for a moment, then fell on his face.

Squat glanced quickly at Raiford's still form, then walked unhurriedly to where the Mexican lay. Kneeling, he took a position where he could keep an eye on Raiford, put his gun carefully on the ground beside him and went through the Mexican's clothes. He pulled out the shirt and found the money belt about Miguel's waist. With a grunt of satisfaction he unbuckled it.

17

RAIFORD OPENED HIS EYES. He felt no pain, but he was numb and cold. The taste of salt was in his mouth. He couldn't see. I'm dead, he thought. Squat—

He heard a grunt and the noise of something moving over

the stones. He blinked his eyes, became conscious of light, and feeling returned to his muscles. He was lying on his right side and about his head was a pool of his own blood. He wasn't dead! Why? Men shot through the head usually die instantly.

Then he felt pain. It was on the right side of his head; that slip he'd made as he whirled had moved him slightly out of line of Squat's gun. He shifted his gaze and saw Squat Armstrong. He was on his knees beside Miguel and was pulling the Mexican's belt from around his waist. That meant that Miguel was dead. And Squat surely thought *him* dead, too.

Raiford saw his gun. It lay four feet away, thrown there by the force of his fall. If he could only reach it! But he couldn't. It would be suicide to try. He'd have to crawl or roll four feet and Squat would be sure to see him move. And Squat's gun was right where he could snatch it in a split second.

Squat thought him dead; the only way to save himself was to convince Squat that he really was dead. If Squat detected a spark of life in him he would finish the job without compunction. How could he keep up the deception?

His right arm was cocked beneath him; he moved his hand towards his face an inch at a time. He turned his wrist and ground his forefinger into a patch of bloody earth. Slowly, his eyes on the busy Squat, he brought the finger to his forehead, pressed it against the white space between his eyes and twisted until he had made a dark round smudge. He dipped the finger into the pool of blood, his blood, and traced the line from the smudge to his temple. Then, slowly and gently still, he moved his hand into its former position.

Squat got up. He had the money belt in one hand and his gun in the other. He glanced sharply at Raiford. The man lay right where he'd fallen; dead as a mackerel, no doubt. Hell, he couldn't miss at that close range.

Squat buckled Miguel's belt about him and walked to where Raiford lay. Holding the weapon in his right hand, he bent over and seized Raiford's arm with his left. He jerked roughly and the inert form rolled onto its back. A pair of blank eyes stared skyward, a smear of blood almost obscured the features. In the midst of the bloody mess was a dark smudge.

"Dead center," muttered Squat. "I said I'd git him and I did."

He nudged the limp form with his boot; it gave a bit, but eyes and face remained blank. Squat knelt down and started searching Raiford's pockets.

Joe held his breath and prayed for the strength to keep his eyes open. He was too weak to think of overpowering this hulk of man; all he could do was to play dead.

Squat took the wallet from his pocket, then gave an animal-like grunt when he found the fat money belt. Roughly he tore it from Raiford's body. He got up and looked for a moment straight into Raiford's eyes. His face was contorted with hate. He leveled the gun at Raiford's head and Joe felt that his end had surely come; then Squat lowered the weapon and spat.

"Hell, you ain't worth another bullet. And I want to show Newt that I only needed one shot."

He turned away and stones rattled beneath his boots as he slouched off. Not for many minutes did Raiford dare to move; then he got painfully to his knees and with his scarf wiped the blood from his face. His gun was gone, taken by Squat, but his horse still stood beside that of Miguel. He got to his feet, swaying, shook off the pain and nausea, and staggered to where the Mexican lay. Miguel was quite dead, and he had died without telling Raiford his secret.

Joe walked unsteadily to his horse and managed to get into the saddle. He must find Miguel's ace in the hole, and he had a strong hunch where Miguel had kept it. Also he was pretty sure that he knew what it was.

His brain was clearing, and as soon as he reached a spring he dismounted and bathed his aching head. There was a ragged tear in the scalp just beneath the brim of his hat, and dry blood had matted his hair. He was a mess, but his strength was returning. He still had his rifle, and now he drew it from its boot and carried it across his knees.

He was alert and he kept as well as he could to cover; but he did not meet a soul on his way to the basin where the cabin was located. He rode completely around it, but there was nobody in the basin and the door to the cabin stood wide open. He hid his horse in a clump of trees and crossed to the shack on foot, his rifle ready. He stood in the doorway looking about the single room, his eyes searching once more for a hiding place; and while he stood there he heard again that jarring thump and this time he knew where it came from.

He leaned his rifle against a wall and went to the table which stood in the middle of the floor. He dragged it to one end of the cabin. The floor was made of twelve-inch boards and he could see the heads of the nails where the planks were spiked to the joists. There was no suggestion of a trap door, but he knew that there must be one. He got his fingers in a crack and pulled, and a whole section of floor came up.

Then his ears caught the sound of galloping hoofs.

He dropped the boards and edged up to a window. Newt Cragg and his five horsemen had entered the basin and were approaching the cabin at a fast lope. He could not get back to his horse without being seen; he hurriedly raised the boards and lowered himself into the hole. When his feet touched ground the floor was on a level with his chin. Carefully fitting the planks in place, he ducked down and let them settle above him.

He heard a stifled groan and, kneeling, felt about him. His fingers found cloth and felt the flesh beneath the cloth give to his touch. He struck a match and saw a man, bound hand and foot and with a gag in his mouth. It was a man he had never seen before, but he knew who it was. A pair of eyes looked up at him in mute appeal.

The ground about them vibrated to the thud of hoofs. Raiford said, "I'll cut you loose, but don't make a sound. If they find us we're both goners."

He got out his knife and severed the fellow's bonds, then removed the gag from his mouth. The sound of hoofs had ceased, but on the floor above them they heard the thump of boots. The man he had freed was moving quietly and Raiford knew he was flexing his cramped muscles.

Newt Cragg's voice came to them. "I can't understand it. Miguel was tipped off sure as hell. And it must have been Lanier who tipped him off. I wish Squat would show up; the Mexican knows every foxhole in these hills, but so does Squat. He could find him for us."

"Mebbe he has," answered one of them. "Mebbe it was him that fired those shots we heard. I figger we oughta stick around here and wait for him to show up. Ain't no fun tearin' around in this kind of country."

A voice came from the rear of the cabin. "Hey, Newt! Here's grub and a stove; what say we throw a meal together while we're waitin'? My belly thinks my throat's been cut."

There were rough words of approval from the others. Raiford heard sounds at the stove and presently there came the crackling of burning wood. The man he had released was crouching beside him, and covered by the noise above them they talked in whispers. What Raiford learned confirmed the guess he had made about Miguel's ace in the hole.

The men above finally gathered about the table, and the sounds of eating reached the two in their hiding place. Then came the scraping of chairs and boxes and the shuffling of feet as the men got up from the table. A voice spoke suddenly.

"Here comes Squat now!"

Again they heard the thud of hoofs followed by the clump of boots. The voice of Squat Armstrong reached them as it rang triumphantly through the cabin.

"Well, fellers, I got 'em! Both of 'em! And only one shot apiece!"

Newt gave an exclamation of pleased amazement. "Miguel and Lanier? Squat, you didn't!"

"I shore as hell did! Been huntin' all over for you. Here's their guns, and here's them fancy spurs Miguel wore, and here's the other feller's wallet. Drilled 'em both through the head. Plumb center. And look, Newt, I reckon me and you got some business to talk over, ain't we?"

"You're right, we have! Clear out, you fellows. Go pick out some nice scenery and look at it."

They filed out and Raiford heard Newt cross the floor. Newt said, "We'll sit at this table, Squat. Got to do some figuring. Take the chair on the other side, partner."

Partner! Raiford grinned in the darkness. Squat was just dumb enough to believe the man.

Chairs scraped as the two sat down on opposite sides of the table.

Newt said, "Now let's see, I paid $500 for the Box L, $100 to Jake Rails, and another $100 in my search for James Lanier. That's $700. There were a few other odd items, but we'll let them slide. Your half of the expenses is $350. We won't figure in the stolen cattle, for the three of us split the proceeds three ways."

"Keno," said Squat. "So far I owe you $350. What I want to hear is how much you owe me. There's Pop Lanier; how much did you get off'n him?"

"I'm getting to that. That old boy didn't have much cash in the house. Probably kept it hidden somewhere. I had a small balance left from what he gave me to pay off the hands."

"I ain't talkin' about that. What I mean is how much did you take off him after you shoved him off the cliff?"

Raiford grasped his companion's arm and squeezed it tightly. The story was coming out and he had another witness!

"I didn't take a cent off him. I didn't go near him."

"Like hell you didn't! How'd you know he was dead?"

"My dear fellow, did you ever take a look at that cliff? Ever notice the rocks at the bottom of that three-hundred-foot drop? I knew he was dead. But I examined him through my field glasses to make sure. His neck was broken."

"You shoulda went through him. How do you know he didn't have a money belt on him? Mebbe that's where all his money was."

Newt's voice was silky. "Did you go through Miguel's clothes? And Montana Joe's? I rather imagine both of them wore money belts."

"We'll git to that. It's yore end of the deal we're accountin' for now. Newt, you come clean. We're partners. I done all the dirty work for you. I fixed Lanier's clock and Abe Ardell's. And now I just got Miguel and that Montana Joe feller. What have you done?"

"Made you a rich man, Squat. I furnished the brains. I could have hired another killer, but where would you get another man with a scheme like mine? And I did the most important job of all. I killed Pop Lanier."

The argument went on, and under its cover Raiford softly raised an end of the trap door ever so little. By turning his head he found that he could see through the crack it made.

He was looking under the table. He could see the feet and legs of the men, and he could see one hand. It was Newt's hand, small and white and graceful, and there was a short-barreled derringer in it. The derringer was pointed squarely at Squat's stomach.

"I ain't denyin' you're smart," came Squat's stubborn voice. "That's why I'm warnin' you now. Don't you try no double-crossin', Newt. I know too much. I could fix yore clock in a hurry if I wanted to."

"I know it, Squat. *Unless I fixed yours first!*"

The gun beneath the table roared once, then a second time.

Newt got to his feet, turned and snatched up the rifle Raiford had left standing against the wall. He had no need for it. Squat got partly to his feet, both hands pressed tightly against his stomach, his mean little eyes wild and staring. Then he fell sidewise, twitched a little, and rolled over onto his back.

Raiford hurriedly lowered the trap door into place. He felt the man beside him grip his arm with nervous fingers. The floor above shook to the tread of the inrushing Box L crewmen and there was a confusion of voices.

"Shut up!" came Newt's sharp order; then, as silence fell, "Yes, I killed him. He threatened me; wanted blackmail for killing Miguel and Lanier. He tried to impress and scare me by admitting that he shot Abe Ardell. I had a gun and I got him under the table. It was just like killing a rat."

Once more the ground shook to the pound of galloping hoofs. One of the crew yelled, "Holy cowbells! Here comes the Double A! I don't want no more of this. I'm gettin' out!"

"Wait, you fool! Squat was a murderer; you got nothing to fear."

"Tell it to the Double A. I got my bellyful of killin'; I shore don't want it full of lead. You boys comin' with me?"

They left the cabin and Raiford heard Newt say, "Run, you cowards! Good riddance."

Then it was Double A boots that shook the floor overhead.

"What's happened?" came Mel Thorne's voice. "Who's that layin' there, Newt?"

The answer came smoothly. "A killer several times over, Mel. Alice, I've just discovered that it wasn't Jim Lanier who killed your father; it was this man here. He bragged about it. And that isn't all. Just a short time ago he shot and killed Miguel Rosas and James Lanier."

"No!" There was anguish in Alice's voice. "Oh, no!"

"I'm sorry, my dear, it's true. Here are Miguel's spurs, and this is Lanier's wallet."

"No," came a voice from under their feet. "That's not James Lanier's wallet. That wallet belongs to Montana Joe Raiford. Cover that skunk, Mel!"

For Newt had taken one look at the face which peered from

beneath the trap door and had reached for the rifle which had been returned to its place against the wall.

Mel was too paralyzed with surprise to obey, but Alice acted instantly. She whipped out the .32 she carried and leveled it at Newt, and Cragg knew by the expression in her face that she would not hesitate to fire. He raised his hands quickly.

"D-don't shoot! Let me explain!"

"Come out, Joe, and listen to the explanation!" Her voice was shrill with relief.

Raiford pushed the trap door to one side and climbed out of the hole. The Double A crew stood transfixed, and Mel Thorne was glaring at him. He smiled wryly at the hotheaded cowboy.

"I don't blame you for wanting to kill me, Mel; but postpone it for a few minutes. I'm not armed."

"You're wounded again!" cried Alice, the gun in her hand wavering. "Oh, Joe!"

"Joe?" repeated Mel Thorne, puzzled.

"That's right. Joe Raiford. Better hold that gun steady, Alice; I see a look of cunning creeping into Mr. Cragg's eyes."

Mel wheeled, his gun whipping up to cover Newt.

"Hold it, Cragg. I sure don't know what this is all about, but if Alice calls this feller Joe, Joe he is."

"Good for you," complimented Raiford. "I'm not James Lanier. And Squat was mistaken when he thought he killed him some nights ago." He turned, bent over the hole and helped the young man out. "This," he said, "is James Lanier. The *real* James Lanier."

18

THE FOUR OF THEM sat on the Double A gallery with the stars smiling down at them. Raiford, his head bandaged, leaned back in his chair. Beside him sat Alice, her hand a willing prisoner in his. Mrs. Ardell rocked gently, her gaze on the little knoll where her husband rested. The real Jim Lanier sat on the edge of the gallery, back against a post.

Looking over the end of the low gallery all four of them could see the bunkhouse, pale in the moonlight, its open door a rectangle of light. The table under the lamp was empty; the nightly game of poker had been canceled by mutual agreement. Instead, the boys still lounged outside in the soft, warm night, discussing the events of the past few weeks and their dramatic culmination that evening.

In a cell in the Calixto jail sat Newt Cragg, his keen mind trying to find a defense against the many crimes for which he would surely be tried. For once his brain failed him; there was no way out. He had pyramided his evil deeds until, topheavy, they had fallen on him and crushed him beneath their weight. He found what consolation he could in the thought that Montana Joe had been lucky. It was poor consolation.

Back on the Double A gallery, Raiford was speaking.

"Yes, that was sure some ace Miguel had in the hole. Towards the end I had a hunch what it was. In the kitchen last night—remember, Alice? You see, Miguel considered himself a gentleman and Newt was too high-handed with him. He thought he'd outfox the lawyer by identifying the wrong man as James Lanier, then holding the real son until he knew what Newt's game was."

"That must have been it," said young Lanier. "After Cragg contacted me, he wrote that he'd have a man meet me at Benson. Dad was such an irritable old fellow that, he said, he wanted to spring me on him at the right moment. I didn't care much one way or the other; he'd driven us from home and hurried the death of my mother and I didn't need the Box L. Got a nice little spread of my own in Wyoming. But I thought Dad might need me, and was getting old, and he was blind. I just had to come down.

"I hit Benson at night and found Miguel waiting for me. I'd known him, so I didn't suspect a thing when he said he'd arranged for me to spend the night with one of his relatives. He turned me over to some of his brigands and they took me to his *rancho*. They treated me well enough, but I was watched all the time and when anybody happened along they tied me up like a sack of grain and hid me under the floor."

He chuckled. "You know, Miguel had a certain sense of humor. I was certainly his ace in the hole!"

"How did you manage to make that thump I heard?" asked Raiford.

"By rocking back on my shoulders and heaving myself upward so that I could kick against the trap door. That first time I tried it I came down on my neck so hard I thought I'd broken it. I didn't repeat the stunt until today. By that time I was so fed up with the thing that a broken neck would have been comparatively welcome."

"It's funny," said Raiford musingly. "I worked like the dickens to get Hurd up in the loft and then to get Newt talking. He had Hurd killed and I had to start all over again. Then I got Miguel's promise to testify against Newt, and Squat promptly shot him. It looked as though my string had run out; and then, when I least expected it, there I was with a perfectly good witness and Newt and Squat baring their souls to each other."

Jim Lanier spoke. "Yeah, you were sure up against it. That Newt Cragg had things worked out to a fare-you-well and within a hair of breaking just the way he'd planned it. If it hadn't been for that stone you slipped on just as Squat fired—! Say,

I got an idea! Find that stone, Joe, break a chunk off it, have it cut and polished and set in a ring for Alice."

"Maybe you have a prior right, Jim. Weren't you and Alice sort of sweethearts at one time?"

"Sure—when we were kids. I even said I was going to marry her when—Holy smokes! I just remembered. I got to go to Calixto the first thing in the morning and send a telegram to my wife! She hasn't heard from me since I left Wyoming. Boy, will she be glad to know I'm coming home!"

"What are you going to do with the Box L?"

"Sell it. Want to buy?"

"Fellow, do I! But I haven't the cash to swing a deal of that size. My ambition was limited to a staunch little cabin, some good horses and cattle and—and—" He faltered to a stop, then finished weakly, "A dog, I think it was."

"You don't need to worry about swinging the deal. I'll make you a good price and give you plenty of time. Shucks, feller, I owe you a whole lot. I might have starved to death in that hole. Well, Mother Ardell, what you say we go inside? Getting kinda chilly, isn't it?"

Mrs. Ardell glanced at the two sitting so close together.

"Well, some folks probably wouldn't notice it. But I'm getting old and you, Jim, have been tied up so long that your circulation probably isn't what it should be." She got up. "Good night, children. Don't catch cold."

There wasn't much danger of that. Alice snuggled a bit closer and Joe slipped an arm about her waist. She looked up at him, her eyes reflecting the soft moonlight.

"What was it you wanted, Joe? A staunch little cabin, some good horses and cattle, and—a dog, was it?"

He looked down at her fondly. "My tongue slipped, honey. What in the world do I want with a *dog?*"